One Night Stand

Shivam Verma

Rajmangal Prakashan

An Imprint of **Rajmangal Publishers**

ISBN : 978-8194617082

Published by :

Rajmangal Publishers

Rajmangal Prakashan Building,
1st Street, Sangwan, Quarsi, Ramghat Road
Aligarh-202001, (UP) INDIA
Cont. No. +91- 7017993445

www.rajmangalpublishers.com

rajmangalpublishers@gmail.com

sampadak@rajmangalpublishers.in

प्रथम संस्करण : अगस्त 2020

प्रकाशक : राजमंगल प्रकाशन

राजमंगल प्रकाशन बिल्डिंग, 1st स्ट्रीट,

सांगवान, क्वार्सी, रामघाट रोड,

अलीगढ़, उप्र. – 202001, भारत

फ़ोन : +91 - 7017993445

First Published : Aug. 2020
Printed by : Thomson Press India LTD & Repro India LTD
eBook by : Rajmangal ePublishers (Digital Publishing Division)
Cover Design : Rajmangal Arts

Copyright © Shivam Verma

Dedication

To friends and family, for being together in thick and thin.

To my amazing publisher for being a pillar of support.

And finally if you are reading this, this is dedicated to you too, yes you. ;)

Preface

Alex is a frolic marketer who hates every relationship with girls that lasts longer than hangovers, which doesn't make him a drunkard. Apart from chasing skirts, he also has a day job he loves. He spends his every weekend, in some of the hip clubs of the city. This too was a weekend, and Alex had just sold some of his sexy ideas to a client, before he hit Floors on Fire, a club popular for hookups and flings.

It is here he meets a fearless journalist Audrey, working on a secret story on the city's drug syndicate. They feel a spark, and the next thing that shakes Alex is waking up next to a dead body. What follows is a network of drug peddlers, hit men, corrupt policemen, notorious criminals, street muscle, media stories, scandals, in Alex's journey to find the killer, while he takes a stand for his innocence.

~~

Table Of Contents

~~

Chapter 1

'Marketing is everyday life with a little bit of lie. Marketing is wildest fantasy come true. Marketing is that hot billboard model that everybody wants, but nobody gets. Marketing is making pocket money look like a billionaire's fortune. Marketing is art of pulling down pants easily, no matter how heavy the wallet is. I believe you don't have to convince a customer to buy a product. You just have to make them feel good about their decision, including the one of visiting you. Marketing is like building faith, like Vatican has done for centuries. They might not be there to make money, but has anyone marketed faith better than them. Every day we hear, C Level executives saying, we are a people's company, we are a people's org. But who are these people, are they us, or its only them. Well, it hardly matters, because point is that they got you thinking about them. Marketing is also like a thinking hat. But some say that it is also the ethos. Really, will you call that Marketing, or Power of Values? I say that it is both. Isn't marketing the power of values? We tell people what we think and what we believe in. For instance, I told a female batch mate of mine that I love dating, I love meeting women, I like hookups, and if the girl is really hot, I also fantasy making out with her. I marketed myself with the values I believe in. Guess what she said, Educated Pervert. But why didn't she bought it, maybe because my values weren't good, or probably because I was talking about my values to a wrong girl'.

This was the highlight of five minute speech on 'Marketing as it should be', on the last day of college. Alex had almost graduated, of course with belief on his skills and knowledge that he would easily excel the exams. Four years of Bachelors in Marketing from the reputed Buffalo

University was no less than a feat. His college gave him education, a worthy degree, and a good job at High Rise marketing agency. The only thing it couldn't give him was the answer on why the girls in his college didn't made him get stories of his days of teenage glory.

Alex liked two things in his life, girls and more girls. As a kid he had grown seeing romance in books, movies, paper columns, and magazines, and he always wondered on why they didn't talked about what happened next. I mean weren't kids supposed to see future as exciting. Love was good to all, but for Alex it was making love, and making more love was the biggest target in this marketing man's life for now.

It has been five months working in High Rise marketing, and never a Friday went by that he didn't hit the 'Floor on Fire' club of the city which was famous for hookups and flings. Alex was getting good at it, for last few times he had almost made it, till a close friend or an ex-boyfriend interrupted in between. Today was Friday, and Alex was hoping high to make it count, except that his female boss Christie was stopping him over working hours for a meeting with a client.

Talking of Christie, she was a single woman in her 40's, as stunning as a CEO could get. Alex had even tried on her, but her wait in life was for a Stock Exchange man who has or who would make millions, buy her a house in Malibu, and get her as many dresses as there were days left in her life. Christie was a tough catch, but today she badly wanted Alex to perform his best, of course in getting that new client on board. It was a vital account for High Rise.

Alex stood there with details of the company, Fast Feast in his hands. He said, "Why doesn't she hits the clubs?"

His colleague Nathan said, "She is not your type Alex. Just look at her. Do you think that she has got that skirt imported from Milan, to be spilled over by a shot of Tequila?"

Alex winced, "Who knows, maybe by something better."

Nathan said, "You are unbelievable. Okay tell me one thing? Have you ever baked muffins?"

Alex exhaled, "Who the hell bakes by themselves now. By the way, does she likes these 'hot' cakes."

Nathan said, "Yes, it is the muffins she would like to end her weekend with, not you."

Alex said 'Whatever'. He moved out from the cubicle, saying goodbyes to the people striding out. The day at office had ended, and what could have been better than asking out Julia on this Friday. Lately confidence level of Alex was reaching newer heights. He was doing good in job, and had a good reputation of being a hard worker. Yes he was a hard worker, only to be realized by Julia who was a junior to her. They had been working together on a new account. Alex turned around, thumbed up to Nathan, and confronted Julia.

Alex said, "Hey are you working late, today?"

Julia said, "Yeah, Christie said to finish these creative. But Its okay, as I love doing my Job with all its thick."

Alex said, "Oh, to quote you. At times even I have worked all night through for High Rise. But I don't complain, till you have amazing colleagues. You know nights are most productive and anything for work."

Julia smiled, "You have a client meeting, need any help?"

Alex said, "Oh, I can handle that. But if you want to help, maybe you can hang out tonight with me. I am going to this club that has a stage show, and you can come with me as my date. If it's okay."

Julia smiled but bleakly, "Sounds good, but I'm not a club person. Plus tonight I am cooking muffins for family."

Alex said, "Muffins, I would love to learn cooking them, but maybe later. Okay. Yeah. Bye".

If Muffin was a person Alex already had committed a crime and killed it cold bloodedly. But seriously who cooks muffins by themselves. Alex thought maybe the country was getting crazy. He doubted that if Nathan was in talks with Julia, or was it too obvious that this girl loves cooking muffins. Alex turned to again look Julia, and all he could admire was nice sleek legs below that skirt that would totally rock the club floor. Alex told himself, maybe she was not the type of girl, or maybe it was meant to be sometime later with this one.

In these four months of work at High Rise, Alex had nailed two awards for the company, bagged cross sales for three accounts, got four referrals from existing accounts, and asked out nine female colleagues. By the way there were only thirteen of them in office, with 3 already married, and one was too fat to adjust in a single bed with Alex.

Christie was changing clothes, yes she was, and it was in the office. Her cabin didn't only had a large mahogany table, chairs, plants, heaps of files and a desktop, but it was a mini studio apartment, with attached bed, wardrobe and a bathroom. Sometimes she slept in office, but alone to the remorse of others. She bathed in office, and often complained of the missing soap bar. Nobody knew who did that. She had many dresses that looked good on her and off her, while today was turn of a special kill at sight dress, as the owner of Fast Feast was 38 year old man and a divorcee. He wasn't a stock guy, but Christie was also cool with a man of family business. Alex entered her cabin, while she was brushing her hairs.

Alex said, "Hey Christie could you please hurry up, client is already here. Hair! Nice hairs, you got a cut."

Christie turned, "No, but I don't wonder on how come you didn't notice it. I mean they are always tied."

Alex tried smiling, "Exactly. You know you are the most good looking boss anyone can ask for, and I believe that someday we would go out when your head is clear, and be more than just a colleague."

Christie dropped her brush on table, "Go out! Yes go out, and shut the door."

Alex always had the burning desire to cross Christie's main office into the studio. In these four months, Alex had fantasized her office bedroom every time he walked in, except for couple of times when he wanted to tie her up with bed and do a High Rise Chainsaw Massacre. Sometimes she was also a bad boss. But really what could be better than sharing a bedroom with your boss in office, it was every employee's ideal office fantasy. Alex prayed that god be liberal on him and fix him up with his boss, while he entered the meeting room.

What a good miracle, he thought, as if God's have heard the prayers, of not him, but of his boss. The owner of Fast Feast was like God coming down straight for her prayers. He looked like a Greek god with great built, decent leather on foots, with a body fit suit. His name was Blake. This handsome man was a pure lady killer with smell of blood coming from his pants. Tonight boss was about to be blown up for sure. He had eyes of hawk, and clam of ocean.

He was an ideal on how every man wanted to look as. Alex felt little jealous, little angry, and little outcasted, as it were men like these that came in between Alex and his manhood glory. Alex thought why didn't he had superpowers to eliminate all good looking men except him in the entire world. Damn, God was mean, and then Christie entered the meeting room. The discussion started.

Alex said, "Fast Feast. There is this girl in her twenties, surrounded by burgers, you know giant burgers with patty coming out from between, hotdogs with a really fat sausages, and finger fries as tickling as they could be, and she is so overwhelmed that she wants to have it all, at same time. Fast Feast."

Blake said with a disapproving voice, "Wait. We are a fast food chain, and we are quite emotional to our customers. This idea doesn't works, not at all."

Christie held his hands and said, "I agree, we have to look beyond those 20's girls. Alex what's next."

Alex turned the PPT and said, "Okay, I have something. There is a family out in a Fast Feast restaurant. The dad is crunching his lettuce studded burger with mayonnaise dropping from other end which is licked by her wife. The kids are playing with Pizza slices by tossing it. Their teenage daughter goes to the counter and takes a plate of nuggets from a nutty store manager who squeezes sauce over it rashly. Ta da. Fast Feast, where families hang out."

Blake said with a disapproving voice, "This is not good, see the kids can't play with Pizza. Its offensive."

Christie held his hands and said, "And the man in there has a huge belly, not good for fast food chain. Next".

Alex gritted his teeth and turned the PPT, "There is a couple in their thirties, and they have planned to live in together to see how compatible they are. The man is quite charming and wants to make her woman feel special. So on first day, man presents the breakfast with bacons and eggs. They eat happily and cuddle. On lunch, the man presents big burgers with French fries and frappe. They eat happily and kiss. On dinner the man presents a bucket of fried chicken and garlic breads. They eat happily and go on to bed half naked. Then the woman says, aren't you forgetting the mayonnaise. The man says, give me a minute. He rushes to a Fast Feast Restaurant. Ta Da."

Blake wasn't completely convinced, but Christie held his hands and said, "I think it's good, and we can try on online channels. You got to give us a chance."

Blake in a low voice says, "I think the chemistry is going to be crucial in this one." They smile.

Alex thought, seriously an online ad, of all this hard work. Obviously Christie didn't took Alex very seriously, but then how could she be holding hands of a man on their first meet, if Christie was that fast she should have been holding something else of Alex. If only Alex didn't had fear of law, this pessimist man would be dead. Alex thought that his first pitch was better, as it was minimalist, not quite as the burgers and sausages were too large, but on a whole it was. But these two blokes with mid age crisis chose the third pitch with all that love and charm. Alex thought but seriously how could a fast food chain have an element of love, it has to be hard hitting.

But in the end who cared, if the man has to rush to a client's store in the end. And Alex was about to be paid good incentives if this account worked well. He made his mind to tell this finalized pitch to Julia and Nathan, to make his point that nobody cooked these days.

Alex was moving out while he entered Christie's office to say a goodbye, and saw her having wine with

Blake. This was unreal. I mean how Christie could do this to Blake and not Alex. Clearly Alex saw that he had have to wait another 6, 7 years to date Christie, but then she would grow too old. The day at High Rise was over, and the next innings in Floor on Fire was to start.

'You are my Knight, Knight, Knight!

This is one of the night, night, night!

Kiss me now, if you might, might, might!

They say I am bad. They say I am broke. They say I got nothing on you.

But you will get to know. They are so right, right, right!'.

This was in own words of Mia. She was an emerging singer of Angelano, our city. She had a huge fan following, and did stage shows every other weekend. She was quite regular to Floor on Fire, and this night she was performing live on her latest single.

Alex always wondered on how the hell a girl as sexy as Mia could be single. Yes she was, and Alex always went up to her to say few good words about the performance in hopes that someday they would exchange numbers. Today she wore a shiny latex dress. It appeared that all stars had draped around her body. For Alex, Mia was the best catch he could ever have in this club, but then it was like catching the stars.

Alex couldn't help but smile to a night that Mia would perform for him exclusive within four walls and get him rolling. He met few of the regulars of the club that sat beside him at the bar table. He would always smile at them thinking it's good to be polite to competitors. Floor on Fire had a female manager named Layla. She was hot, she was single, and greeted Alex well every time he visited. The only thing that came in between Alex and Layla was that she had seen too many flings to be hit by one. Alex always thought on why girls were always so judgmental.

Layla said, "Hey Champ, so who is gonna be the lucky girl tonight?"

Alex smiled, "I swear, my astrology says, it will be a girl with name starting with L. Isn't yours too."

Layla said, "Oh, that's sweet. But there goes way to girl's L area, ah lounge area. Keep trying though."

Alex chuckled, "Wait. I need to ask you something. You don't have a boyfriend, you don't make out, but you work in hippest club of Angelano. Why? I mean what do you expect of a man? Does he have to make muffins, or write a new song about pseudo relationship like Mia? Why there always have to be strings attached?"

Layla cleared her throat, "I love working here, because I like loud music, and it also keeps me deaf to all those petty proposals. And boy, it's good to have strings attached, or there would be no fun in pulling them down."

Layla laughed wickedly and Alex thumped his heart, "You always kill me with your words."

Alex got moving to find her right girl. It was not every time that Alex got lucky in Floor on Fire, but it was the place most likely to get lucky. This club was always on full house with girls, and boys too but wait who would come here to see boys. Without any bed on floor this was the best place in city to get laid. The only thing that could stop you was hitting on wrong girl. The music was always loud here, but it didn't stopped Alex to seek hearing a yes, a yes, and a yes. Tonight the floor was really on fire, with all those minis the club was looking like a half pant meat shop. There has to be someone to die for tonight.

Mia today was extra busy, signing off autographs. Alex saw a girl in white. She was wearing an off the shoulder top and a draped skirt. Her chest was shining and pulling Alex for a kiss. She was quite styled for the night, and apparently she visited clubs once in a while. Today must have been some special day. It was maybe a birthday, or college graduation, or a new job, as she looked over 22, 23. She was surrounded by girls, and just two men with other girls, that two men made the difference, because if she was seeing somebody, that some man should've been around, but was not. White meant, she was clear headed and would not build up too many things in mind. She was drinking either gin or vodka, so one had to careful on how to stretch the conversation, but Alex wasn't worried about how to put up a thing or two.

Everything looked perfect, if only she didn't turned out to be nun. Yeah, the nuns also wear white, and she could have been a fashionable nun, after all anything was possible in city of Angelano. Alex held his pants tight, made a move, and stood beside her.

He peeped and said, "Ah, that is Billy Marlow without any doubt."

One girl smiled and said, "That is right! But I am sorry you are."

Alex broadly said, "I am Alex, and since I've moved in I've made it my passion to know everything about city."

Alex continued with a poker face, "Did you knew that Billy had one of the best sex lives in Angelano. Do you know he has woken up with more girls than he had slept with? Any idea how? Well because if you have a girl by your side, who needs to sleep. While some people say he has magic in his pants, but I wonder if that magic doesn't belonged to Abra Ka Dabra. But, but, all who had know him always had a sound sleep."

They laughed and another girl exclaimed, "Didn't knew that, though he was close to my father."

~~

Chapter 2

That girl in white dress was Anna. Yes it was her graduation day, not exactly as she had graduated a day before, and here she was celebrating with her friends. Those two guys were not even boyfriends of any of them, they were batch mates, as clearly as one of the girls quoted. Tonight Alex had hit it right, as Anna was carefree and was also liking his company. They were drinking vodka shots on every high note of their talks. The girl whose father was Billy's friend couldn't believe this entire time that Billy was a hole digger, but our Alex piled up heaps of lie to support it.

Mia on the other hand had again started singing on huge public demand. It was a dance track and Alex took the full opportunity of taking Anna to the dance floor. Alex had Anna in his arms, while his eyes were checking out Mia's latex dress. Seriously no straight man in Angelano could resist fantasizing about a girl dressed in Latex skirt. It was grossly sexy. Alex swayed Anna in her arms, every time Mia's eye would fall on dance floor. Mia did noticed him, but overlooked, and that was okay for Alex, as he was saving these eye encounters for the next time he met Mia. Alex knew that the first rule of getting laid in a night was to speed up things. Meeting, drinking, and now dancing, were all going good with speed.

Next was to start an intimacy, so he thumped a couple of times on Anna's butts instead of her back pretending like a bad shot, and she freakily smiled. That signal was good enough for Alex. A thump on butt liking girl is all what you need. Then a romantic number got started playing, and Alex in his mind was already stabbing the DJ for having played such song for first time, since he had stated visiting this club.

Well but it was a blessing I disguise, as Alex could have used it as a backdrop to kiss her. But that would ruin his plans, he took Anna by her arms and got back to the tables.

Alex said, "I think white looks sexy on you. Wait, you will look even sexier without this white. I mean the color."

Anna smiled, "Yeah I know, I've been told, but this time I want to see myself without a white."

Alex chuckled, "Oh, trust me you will. Why don't i take that white, and then take a picture of you."

Anna laughed lightly, "Well that sounds perfect, only that it won't be you but Hailey."

Alex drew himself back, "I thought you and I were going to take the elevator, to take this up to someplace nice."

Anna twisted his cheeks, "You are cute, and I'd love to make out with you. But I am a Lesbian."

Alex took a long breath, "It's okay, you two can do your thing, while I will do mine."

Anna snapped, "Alex that doesn't happens with us, I mean we two, not you. So Bye!".

Alex couldn't believe himself, while Anna walked away in the same white that had made his eyes go round. He thought to himself, Lesbian, ugh. There was only one word in his head, Lesbian. He looked around the club, and saw two women hugging, then on other corner a woman was kiss greeting another woman. On the bar table, Layla was laughing loudly while a woman was explaining her something. He thought if anything gross than this had happened to him. But couldn't, and how could he ask her after that for a threesome.

He took two shots of Tequila, and closed his eyes for a little mediation. How could a marketer as good as him pick such wrong girls, was it the plan of god. He imagined shoving knives in belly of Senator Jason Bishop who had recently legalized same sex relationships. He is the one who empowered girls like Anna to refuse a hot pick like Alex. He said to himself, God what was happening with all hot chicks of Angelano, and will this freaking club ever get me laid.

A voice came from behind, "Hey, can you please pass the napkin. Fuck this mayonnaise is all over me."

Wait, what, Mayonnaise. Alex couldn't help but smile. Maybe the gods have listened. He turned around and got struck with the first look of that girl who was trying to get rid of most beautiful thing man could ever make, wait the fast food chains had ever made. She was wearing a strapless top and a flared skirt. He thought thanks god the dress was black and not the lesbian white. He slowly turned around to see the club, and couldn't find any one more pretty than her, then his eyes fell on latex dress of Mia. Okay one or two exceptions were always there. The girl then waved her hands on Alex's face. That was check, wait she couldn't be assistant of Blake who had come in to check the chemistry of that ad. Alex slowly took the napkin and gently started wiping the beauty, the mayonnaise.

The girl said, "Oh, I can do that. I was eating a burger while way in and a blind cockhead bumped in to me."

Alex swallowed his saliva, "Oh this place is full of them, I wish they kept cock and head separate."

The girl just felt something really odd being said, and why wouldn't be that, as it was our Alex. She gently smiled, while they both worked on removing that beauty, that mayonnaise from snake black colored dress. The stain couldn't completely go, but Alex took her to the nearest table. The night soon would be over in club, and he always remembered the first rule of getting laid in one night, speed up. They drank to new acquaintanceship.

The girl said, "So why you are here, in this club. What brings you?"

Alex snapped, "Oh it's my job. I save girls from Mayonnaise. I am the White Man, the hero of every woman's dream. That's me. What about you."

The girl laughed and said, "Oh, well I am an investigative journalist, but you can't tell anyone."

Alex smiled as he had won half of the battle. You can't tell anyone, Woah! The girl trusts you, and this is the first emotion vital for getting laid in one night. Trust, because trust was the thing that thursts women from bar table to hotel rooms. The first battle was won. But then Alex thought that she was a journalist. For him the only thing that needs to exposed this night was to be this girl from her black dress, and not the purpose of his visits to club.

Alex hesitatingly asked, "So, I guess you must be here to cover the food. Let me help you. Once I treated a girl in this restaurant, guess what. She puked the entire night, and next day his father was at my doorstep with a gun. You know, this place is cursed. But their hotel is good, private, cozy, and pretty clean."

The girl smiled, "Sounds like some plans. But I am here to do the biggest story of my life."

Alex said, "Girl you are spot on. Great things happen when you are with great people."

The girl got Alex closer, "A very big drug deal is going to happen tonight in this club, and I will uncover it."

Alex thought on why did it always happened to him, and this was just enough for a night. First a lesbian, then a lady bond on a mission. Well, Lady Bond sounded good, as there is lots of sex in one night, but then the title Bond is the one who gets to screw, not the other people around. And this girl was looking someone who would screw. He remembered his gods and all those books on flings that never had any tips on how to deal with a journalist on mission, as all of them were written by some or the other journalist. And this girl was little scary. Then the girl took her handbag and showed Alex a glimpse of a gun. The nightmare got true, he got scared and felt like a tiny weeny.

Alex said, "Hey hold on. Why don't you tell the police, and let them do their jobs. Why all this trouble?"

The girl said, "Police can't be trusted. These people have bought many policemen, and will not stop."

Alex said, "I thought I was the white man. But nope, you are. I think we should change your dress to white."

A call came to girl's cellphone and she said, "Hey, I have to go. But see you around, I am not leaving."

Alex thought, I am not leaving, so neither am I, the night is on. This girl in black with beauty of mayonnaise turned out to be just another girl he had bumped into in this club. Also she admitted to have bumped into a cock head. Did she accept that as her fate for tonight? She did look intelligent, educated, and wise, to have realized god's greater plans. Yeah, he said to himself and turned to gaze

Mia, who was now sitting in front seat listening to other artists. Her latex dress was looking tighter while Alex's pant was loosening. It came to Alex's mind that maybe he should follow his pants, after all pants are the best explorer.

But marketer inside Alex said, its not right time to hit Mia. After all she was a micro celebrity, and could possibly throw tantrums. Maybe after Alex got a decent hike, a nice promotion, couple of awards, a cozy apartment with bigger bedroom and a luxury sedan, was the best time to ask Mia out, if any normal person was to say, but Alex had a whole new theory of the right timing to ask Mia out, that was when her music tracks failed in selling copies and she was forced to do back to back stage shows in Floor on Fire, to be finally be so exhausted to take a break, that was when Alex would come in. It occurred to Alex, that maybe on next Friday he should gift Mia a brand new latex dress, and tell her 'It's for you, but you must know that you will also look good without it'. That was just perfect. He deviated his attention to find another right pick before night ended. He saw a hot girl sitting idle at the bar, gazing on the floor, possibly for men.

Alex approached and said, "You know, if you want a man, look at other men. It always works, as you can see. By the way, I am Alex. It's better to know the name first."

The girl grinned, "Oh, I was looking at my dad, he just went that side. Didn't expected him here."

Alex said, "Ha. I got this. He is probably here with his girlfriend. Can't dad's play dingy dongy. Come on."

The girl sighed, "He is a convict, got out from jail tonight, and he has gone that side chasing my boyfriend."

Alex nodded while his stay away alert has already rang in his head. He gulped the drink in his hands and went towards floor asking the girl whether it was the same direction, and soon vanished in the crowd. Why did this happens all the time to me, Alex thought, One night, one lesbian, one journalist on a mission, and one daughter of a mad convict, all for the same night.

Alex always believed that god had great plans for him, and his belief was getting stronger. What the hell was wrong with girls of Angelano. Did this city didn't had one girl who would appreciate relationships wrapped in one night. After all they would save time for another relationship, another man. Alex thought that maybe career in Soft Skill training was a jackpot idea for Angelano. It occurred to his mind that maybe call in for a friend. That was a good idea. He would not only share drinks with him, but also get a wing man.

Alex called Nathan, "Hey Nathan. Why don't you come down to Floor on Fire and we do the brother thing, the night is on me. Anyways you don't have plans for tonight."

Nathan in a slow voice said, "I am with some girl, can't come now. Sorry!".

Alex chuckled, "Hey you little prick, whom did you bump into."

Nathan exhaled and said, "I am at Julia's house, making muffins with her. She called me over."

Alex yelled, "What? You double faced pig, how can you do that to me? You are dating Julia, and making muffins. I knew it, you always had a bad eye on her dresses, and tonight you will rip them apart. You know what say that again. The word, the sorry, you owe me a big one."

Nathan said, "Okay sorry. Oh my god, I just poured little extra sugar syrup. Call you later."

Alex wanted to scream, but the music was too loud that he himself wouldn't listen. Four months, Nathan chewed the same burger with him, and how could he eat muffins with Julia at her place. Nathan just took away that chance to spoil dresses imported from Milan. Alex never went to Milan, so how could have drawn funny poses on the historic walls of the city.

Julia was his only chance to smudge Milan with his manhood. And Julia, that wicked girl who always acted like she still had her sweet tooth, told him that she was cooking Muffins for family tonight, and since when Nathan became her family. People at High Rise were all bigots, except Alex as he came to a conclusion. Alex made his mind that next time Julia came for help to him for creative ideas, he would unzip his pants and show her his boxers that were more stylish than her dresses, of course with sub titles. Night was upon end, Alex took few more drinks, and thought of leaving and catching up with a movie or something on his couch. He got headed to doors and got bumped in to a girl.

Alex saw her and said, "Tonight you are cursed, and you will keep bumping into cockheads. Only if you see above the cock and below the head, my heart, you might free yourself from this curse. Ta. Da."

Girl laughed, "God, you are such a sight. I already feel relaxed seeing you."

Alex chucked his tongue, "Save the expression for tomorrow morning when we'll rise together. By the way what happened to that drug deal? I hope nobody follows us and we rise with some third person."

Girl sighed, "Ah, my source has ditched me. He was supposed to meet me here. Anyways the deal will happen, or might be happening, but I've lost my great story."

Alex said, "This is what happens when you choose a wrong man. Come with me."

They went to the bar table and drank couple of drinks. Both had got too drunk for the night. Meanwhile Mia was again on stage on public demand singing her maiden track. Girl had listened to her for the first time and was so impressed that wanted to take her autograph. But Alex refused to walk up to Mia, after all how could he walk up to her future date with a present date. But was spoiling the present for future worth it? Of course it was, Latex was forever, it was strong, it could stretch over a period of time, and it was all that a man would want.

So they sat there while Alex told her wild things about himself, and how worthless he felt for over pricey dresses of women, as their glory lasted till the woman met the right man. He told her about his marketing skills, on how he could sell a sex toy as a Christmas gift. He told her about the other women he met tonight, and thought that you were the craziest of them, as how could one uncover a drug deal in a shady club where every other man is in possession of drugs. He told her that he had a fantasy about sleeping with a female author, because they claim that they are good with pen which Alex had a disbelief with. They drank more and more, with more secrets coming out from other person.

Girl said, "Phew. You've told me so much. But haven't still asked my name, you know. Ha ha."

Alex snapped back, "You know, name is what our parents want us to be. But the question is what do you want to be tonight. Sexy Mia, or Hunter Queen, or Teddy Bear, or Wild Bear or a courageous Cougar?"

Girl interrupted, "Stop it, your suggestions are disgusting. By the way, you can call me Audrey. Its my name, and i can be whatever I like to be with this name."

Alex smiled, "So Audrey, what will you want tonight for desert, maybe some whipped cream."

Audrey said, "I can't believe I am doing this. But I can try some of that."

Both left the bar table, hanging by each other's shoulder. Alex was on a new high that finally all this time of hitting Floor on Fire had finally bore him fruits. He felt like a winner, and wanted to call Christie, Julia, Nathan, and many others to see him do this thing tonight. But then he was also little mad at the fact that he had drank too much and feared if he didn't last the night. But seriously, this was what Alex wanted, no long lasting things. But one or two exceptions were always there. They moved towards the hotel section that was attached to the club. Alex said to the reception that they wanted a room. He told them that they were couples, and had lost keys to their home. After a little more explanation, that they were too drunk to drive and be caught by policemen for drinking and driving, the hotel boy was escorting them to their room.

The room was big and had lots of space to play and pose around. Alex was so drunk that he told the hotel boy to lock the room from outside, as they were going nowhere else, and no one could come in between. Not even that latex dress of Mia. Yes Mia, if you were some how listening it, then Alex had loud out to say that he would prefer a mayonnaise stained dress over a brand new latex one. Alex started saying softly A for Alex, A for Audrey, B for Bed, and C for I close my eyes. Audrey had jumped over him and started taking off her clothes. Alex got struck for a minute, that he had seen the bra Audrey was wearing, but got calmed as he remembered peeping into her breasts when they were having drinks.

Alex yelled, "My name is Alex, and I want to be everything that I want tonight with Audrey."

~~

Chapter 3

Was it morning? Alex couldn't tell with his flickering eyes, but quickly remembered himself of the feat he has achieved. One night stand after a long it was. Alex smiled to all the stories he was going to tell to Christie while she kept waiting for her stock man, to Julia who could never get creative despite wearing designer dresses from Milan, to Nathan who no matter tried hard could never learn how to make good muffins. Alex held his head, thinking how to say a goodbye to Audrey. He thought of saying, Audrey you know what the drug deal happened as I felt on a new high, and probably we should respect the addiction of it and do this often.

He turned and saw the bare back of Audrey, which was godly. Alex spread his arms around her to find the bed sheet to be wet. He thought, Yeah I can sweat a woman, didn't knew that. He turned Audrey into his arm to realize her body was bleeding. Alex yelled WTF. The hangover was gone, and he fell back on his feet only to see that Audrey was murdered. He touched her nerves and they were as blank as the night he tried remembering. Did I do it? Alex couldn't believe on how this happened. There was a deep wound in her belly. Probably it was a work of sharp knife.

Alex's eyes fell on a packet of Drugs lying beside her body. Alex's head was spinning. The drug dealers killed her, but how was he going to explain this to Police that was already corrupt. Someone knocked at the door.

The voice came in, "Sir, its housekeeping. Please let me in."

Alex knew that it wasn't the best time to be seen with a dead body. He panicked and went for the door. He opened it, and saw Housekeeping lady panic only to realize that his hands were still smudged with blood. He pushed the lady and ran along the corridor faster than he took things to get laid in a night.

Alex was talking to himself, 'I don't think she saw me. I was too quick. Plus women don't remember my face well. Yeah, that's right. But only hot women do that, not fat women. Okay. Calm down'.

Plan was simple, nobody had seen Alex till now with body. So he could probably sneak out of the city and maybe stay in some hotel in country side, drink some cheap wine, and no more hitting on women, till police caught the killer. But wait, the Police was corrupt. Audrey had told that many policemen are on their side. But the there are also good people in world. Not everyone sees a mini skirt as meat shop window, some do praise the fashion behind it. Whatever, Police had to catch the real killer. Alex was riding on a cab to his home, while driver was getting suspicious.

Driver asked, "Hey man, it's quite late for a cab drive. Did boss hold you up?"

Alex snapped, "I wish, but she likes older men. I mean. Hey look I was with my date and I do this often."

Driver didn't asked any further. Obviously he had sensed that Alex was a womanizer. The home was near, and Alex heard Police siren sound. He got scared, and looked out from window to see that Police was already at his doorstep. His landlord was standing in shorts talking with an officer. Alex told the driver to pull ahead towards market. Shit! Alex thought. Police knew, but how come so fast? Alex was sure that he was being framed for the murder. Now what would happen?

Probably another Police car must've reached his home town address. Since when did Dating turned so horrific. Well technically it wasn't dating but one night stand, but then that too hasn't to be deadly. Alex was murmuring, Floor on Fire, Floor on Fire, my life is on Fire. Alex couldn't imagine him being sent to prison. Prison really, they had no girls, but gay criminals. The player in outer world often became prey in prison. No way, Alex thought that he would never give up his integrity to a rowdy gay leader of criminals.

But what were the options, only one, to prove himself innocent. Yes, if fantasizing women was a crime, then he was a criminal, if hitting on hot chicks was a crime, then he was a criminal, if offering drinks to lonely women was crime he was criminal, if planning to gift a Latex dress to a girl was crime he was, but murdering a girl was not a crime, he thought not a crime he committed. Alex went into a café in the market which was huge enough to hide in a corner.

Obviously Alex needed help, so he thought of people to contact. The first call he decided to make was to Edward. He was more of a professional friend. No not the criminal types professional, as Alex was not that type, nor was he proved guilty yet. Edward worked in Angelano Chronicle and helped Alex for PR campaigns.

Edward said, "God Alex! Where are you? Police is looking for you in whole town. Tell me you didn't did this."

Alex snapped, "Of course. I like to sleep with women, not get them to sleep forever. I am being framed."

Edward said, "My junior is covering your case. He is at the Hotel Sheldon co-ordinating with police. You know, Police has too many evidences against you. The strangest one is, that Police has found traces of your semen on bed sheet, but not in Audrey's body. They believe you have masturbated after killing her."

Alex felt disgusted, "God that is sick. You know I can't do this, no matter how sexy the dead body is. I mean no."

Edward said, "My boy has told me that Police has also found that girl was drugged and they have found a packet of drug besides her body with sign of city's drug syndicate. They also know that girl was there to uncover the drug syndicate. Now they think you are their boss, the infamous drug lord".

Alex yelled, "Is police retarded. I don't even know what brown sugar is, is it really brown. Well I know it is not brown, but I hope you get my point. Drugs no, Sex yes, and that is about it."

Edward said, "Listen, in short you are in deep trouble. They have an invincible case against you."

Alex despairingly said, "Didn't knew trouble could also be deep. But I will prove myself innocent."

Edward said, "That's my boy. Listen, I'm there for help, but please call me from some other number. Okay."

Alex realized that he has to be smarter. He immediately switched off his phone. There was no one around. Alex thought on how did his semen was found on bed sheet and not in Audrey's body. Did he slept with the bed sheet rather than on it. God, this was so confusing for Alex. Too much was happening with him. Only time he had imagined for too much was a wild fantasy of sleeping with twin sisters at one time. This really was deep trouble.

God, his senses had failed him, as why didn't stay away alert rang the first time she said that she was a journalist, but back then she sounded like a James Bond girl, and now his lives had got those double 'o', one a murder, and another being a drug lord. One thing was clear that after he passed over, probably Drug Lord found Audrey and killed her, in fear that she might not find him in near future. The killer was drug lord, and this lead was enough for now.

Alex called Nathan from a pay phone in café. Nathan said, "Good God that you are safe. What all has happened Alex. I always told you to get rid of chasing ladies."

Alex said, "I don't know what is happening, and where will this go. But I didn't kill her."

Nathan said loudly, "Bro you are not a lady killer, I know that, everyone at High Rise knows that."

Alex too repeated loudly, "Yes, I am not a lady killer, I was never a lady killer. I never got laid. Fuck why did I went to that shady club ever."

Nathan said, "Oh not like that. Well you know Christie has shown her true colors. She has disbanded you from High Rise. Right now Police is searching your cabin in office."

Alex angrily said, "She always orders meatballs with noodles, right. I will give her a new taste of it. Once I get out from this hell created by some drug lord."

Nathan said, "Hey Julia is coming. Listen bro, I am always there if you need any help. Okay."

Alex felt speechless, on what on earth was Julia doing with Nathan. Had they moved in, or did Nathan add whipped cream on those muffins. What the hell was wrong with girls of Angelano, all missed what the real deal in life was, like this Audrey who was supposed to live a normal life, and not chase drug deals. Till this moment there was only one Lord in Alex's life, that was almighty above us all, but now drug was attached to it, like those strings he always hated. His eyes fell on TV that was running breaking news, and obviously it was about Alex, Audrey and the drug syndicate. Alex always wanted to be famous, but not like this.

Detective Joe Winslow was on air and making statements that Angelano Police had finally found a lead to Leader of city's drug syndicate, and it was Alex. Then Alex's picture got flashed, and it was one hung in his bedroom that he had got clicked in a strip club with almost naked woman surrounding and clinging to him. God, Alex thought that this moronic police got only this picture to flash on National TV. Already his success rate of getting women sleep with him was low, and after the girls of Angelano saw this picture his chances were to die.

Joe continued saying that this man is a womanizer, and would do anything for sex and drugs. Then a footage of him staring Mia, his thumping of Anna's butt, him hitting the girl of convict, and him talking with Audrey flashed. Christie too appeared on TV saying that this man Alex was so sick that he always stole the soap she bathed with. Alex held his head, as if everyone was trying to have a piece of him. The story wasn't over, his parents appeared on TV saying, my boy can't kill a woman, because he would rather do other things with her, now excuse me. Alex felt a little happy, but felt awkward as Dad could have quoted it better.

His key to get out from this accusation of murder was catching the drug leader, or perhaps the person who was doing the drug deal that night. But who could tell him about all those things. Audrey was dead, and he had no shady friends that could be of help. All of his friends were only good at fixing him up for a date. His head clicked.

He called Layla, and she said. "Alex, Alex. What all is this. You killed a woman as she didn't sleep with you."

Alex snapped, "Technically she was killed after we slept together, and you can't believe all of this. You know I could get a woman by hook or crook, but not on a knife point."

Layla exhaled, "I know, but how will you prove your point. All evidences are against you."

Alex said, "I have a plan. I will catch the drug lord and make him confess this crime. I know it will not be an easy road, that's why I need your help. Please tell me Layla, who circulates drugs in Floor on Fire. I know you know it."

Layla hesitated, "It could cost me my life, if I get in all this trouble."

Alex snapped back, "You are already dead. You don't date, you don't make out, what is there in your life. I mean, come on, I know how to keep things secret, even if you slept with me, I won't tell anyone."

Layla said, "Phew, you are unbelievable. His name is Terry. But he is a small time peddler of this club."

Alex noted all details, and knew Terry was the man. It might be that, on night of murder this Terry was doing the drug deal, and he could also have killed Audrey. Even if he didn't, then his job of being drug peddler would have him known the drug lord of city. Either way meeting this man was a good go. Meeting a man, god, Alex couldn't remember last time he was chasing a man, and it was all because of crazy girls of Angelano.

Only if Anna wasn't a lesbian, they would have make out and moved on, and he wouldn't have met Audrey and all of this wouldn't have happened. Or maybe it was marketing as it shouldn't be. Maybe Alex was doing it all wrong. Maybe wrapping up relationships in one night was wrong, and he shouldn't be chasing girls to bed in time shorter than their pants. Alex felt for the first time that his following pants could also lead you to shitty situations. It was early morning, and meeting Terry now was good time, as he sure would've returned to his home by now and be sleeping. Terry lived in Meat Market. This place was quite infamous for all things shady and illegal. Alex took the transit rail while wearing a long pullover, hiding his face, and stopped at the Meat Market station. It was a huge market where you would find all sorts of meat in bulk including fishes. Till this point he had only seen women as meat shop, but now the real deal was happening in his life.

The butchers were staring Alex, as if they knew he was the killer. Seriously, Alex thought do they only stare while they should be selling their stuff. This must have been next level marketing to make buyers scare enough to buy from them. Alex had walked long and hadn't seen one normal man without knife whom he could ask directions to Terry's house. He just preferred to stay away from knives as one had already stirred trouble in his life. He finally found the building that had Terry's apartment. It was and old construction, while the alley had many young men taking drugs, injecting in their veins. This was the right place Alex had to be, not because he was recently promoted to the drug lord, but it was here he could catch the killer. Alex knocked on his door.

Terry showed up and said, "Hey what do you want, I don't sell drugs from my home."

Alex smiled and punched him in face. He got in and said, "I know you killed Audrey."

Terry wiped his face and said, "Are you high. I don't kill people, they die themselves with my drugs."

Terry was casual and yes he had just risen from bed. It didn't appeared that Terry had killed Audrey. He roamed about his apartment searching for something, and then he threw today's newspaper on Alex's face. IT had a cover story of Audrey's death with a picture of Alex besides it. Terry looked back and grinned.

Alex said, "Listen, I know she was there that night trying to uncover a drug deal which makes you a part of it. Now give me the name of your Drug Lord or the killer. You have two options, either I will give you the money for this tip, or I will call the police right now from my mobile and we both go to Jail. It doesn't ends here. I have made lot of money in my life and my lawyers will make sure that you take your last breath within prison walls."

Terry laughed, "Why don't I give you a shot of Cocaine. You know it is better than those girls."

Alex yelled shoving Terry into the chair, "This isn't funny you faggot. Maybe I should make some calls."

Alex was bluffing like he always did with girls he hit, but it also worked on a man. Terry was calming him down, and went in to the kitchen asking him if he needed coffee. Alex didn't say anything, and looked around in his apartment, which clearly wasn't cleaned for months. Alex wasn't sure if he said the right things but his guts told that Terry couldn't have killed Audrey. He was a small time prick, a prick that maybe upgraded with a murder. No, No.

Terry came back and said, "You know Bob Marley. Of course you do. I am more like him. Live and let live. Trust me. Okay see that cockroach in my kitchen. I haven't killed even that, and you say that I killed Audrey."

Alex looked at the cup of coffee he was offered, and imagined cockroaches making out in it. He felt puking, but didn't showed. He slid the cup of coffee towards Terry, reached for his pocket, and took out handful of hundred dollar bills, and placed it below the cup of coffee. Alex looked back at Terry.

Terry gulped a sip of coffee, "I will need more of it, and you will have to do something for me. Just few blocks away from here is Chinatown. I used to sell them drugs few months back, but then I cheated them and now they are after my life. Recently they have put a word out in Meat market for a demand of kilos of cocaine. It's a huge deal, I can't miss it, neither can I show up to sell them, or they'll kill me. So you will do that deal for me."

Alex smelled the coffee and said, "I hope this is coffee only."

Terry said, "I know it sounds weird, but in brotherhood you help someone and they help you."

Terry convinced Alex that on the night Audrey was killed he had no drug deal happening there and he never did drug deals in such high end places. He admitted that he did sell drugs to club members and on that night he did sell drugs to few people, but came back to home.

He also told Alex that area was not under his control, and there were other drug dealers handling that club. He would tell their names only after Alex did this deal. Terry had won trust of Alex, now it was Alex's turn. Hitting women was easier, Alex thought, as only the trust of women mattered, but this was brotherhood, more of an Anna's thing. One drug deal had already put his life in troubled waters, and he hoped high that this drug deal took it out from that.

Police had already made him a criminal, Alex thought, and now terry was making him act like them. It was funny that he had to do crime, in order to prove himself innocent. He already felt like a criminal, but then women also always faked orgasm. It would be over soon, he thought.

~~

Chapter 4

The deal with people from Chinatown had to happen tonight. As Alex anyways didn't had any place to go, especially night clubs or even High Rise office, so Terry gave him refuge for the entire day, as he knew it all. Alex couldn't believe the fact that he was now a partner with a drug peddler. During the day, two teenage girls dropped by Terry's house to buy some cocaine, and asked Alex if he would like to party. Guess what Alex responded, that he was a gay. He finally realized that being gay or lesbian was not always a choice but also circumstantial, and he shouldn't have seen Anna with prejudice.

Wait, was it that Anna wanted to avoid sleeping with Alex that she said that she was a lesbian. Anything was possible especially with girls of Angelano. As the day passed many people dropped by Terry's house to buy drugs and he gave them too. Alex couldn't understand on why did Terry open his house doors to him telling he didn't sold drugs at home, and gave these people the stuff. Alex knew that girls didn't always wanted him, was it the same with men too. He looked in the mirror and as always looked awesome, then what was it.

Anyways, Alex was now thinking what if he got caught by Police during this Chinatown deal. If so, no one in this world would be able to save him. Well not exactly, he knew that even one good lawyer is better than 10 hot girls in lying. Yes lying, not laying. But what if the Chinatown people killed him suspecting he was a man of Terry. Alex got scared for a while, but why should he have been. He was a good marketer, and if a marketer cannot sell a thing or close a deal, then it was better to blamed for a murder, because least he had murdered marketing. Alex felt good. The night was on, and it was now his turn to prove his brotherhood. How gay that sounded, Alex thought.

Terry was busy in his bedroom. Yes he was busy and without a girl. Apparently men unlike Alex could get busy in bedroom even without a girl. He came out with a bag, a black bag. Obviously it was filled with packet of drugs. He kept that on the table right in front of Alex. It didn't looked heavy, but it was as it held the weight of gayish brotherhood, along with weight of Alex's first official crime.

Terry saw little misty sweat on Alex's face and asked, "Are you sure you can do this?"

Alex whiffed, "Does it looks like I am dealing with drugs for the first time. Huh. How about the newspaper you threw at me, didn't you read the piece. I am city's drug lord."

Terry laughed, "Listen, his name is Chih Ming Ho. He talks less, and gets straight to the point. You just have to make him sure that you are not Police nor DEA nor some enemy gangster. Rest will work fine. Tell him that Azrock told you about this deal, and if he buys now, he would get good deals in future. Getting it?"

Alex snapped, "Hey stop it. All my life I have made men fool and women fooler. Don't worry."

Alex took the bag and got on his way out. The butchers of Meat market were still staring him. Okay, it had just started to look weird, as Alex wasn't wearing a latex dress, nor was he a chick. The butchers were also staring at his bag which he thought was even more important than his life which was going to end in a prison if this deal didn't worked. But there was this one thing that Alex couldn't understand on why Terry made him do this deal. Obviously he wasn't a loner, though Alex was sure that there were no women in his life except few odd customers, then why didn't he did this deal with one of his friends. Of course the Chinese must have known all of his friends or else why would he risk giving him kilos of cocaine. Everything was working as planned.

Alex had also taken a cab to Chinatown, then his mind struck with advise he had given that night to Audrey. 'Why don't you tell the police, and not take all this trouble'. Seriously, why was Alex doing this, when he could easily convince the Police that this drug peddler knew about the real drug lord. Police was corrupt but not all of them. Alex reached for his cellphone and typed 911, Should he call or not? It was the exact feeling he got when in dilemma of calling his one night stand girls again. Then the cab driver told him that they had reached the destination. The climax of this fake crime had reached. Guess now it was only brotherhood Alex had to do.

The Chinese were standing in line in that abandoned building in Chinatown. It looked like Bruce Lee movies, with gunmen wearing odd clothes, and holding guns of mass destruction. Alex thought, it would have been better if this all looked little more like Jackie Chan movie, as it had suited men, some humor and couple of women too. Behind him was the street of Chinatown and few food stalls serving fried octopuses. Seriously octopuses, who ate them, maybe sharks, but really not normal men. The tentacles of octopuses were still tingling as Alex saw. This felt very deadly, maybe it was a sign that Alex hopped back in the cab. But was too late, the cab was gone.

Alex said, "Hola! I mean Sayonara, oh to the cab driver. Ni Hao gentlemen."

A fat man gestured another and he checked Alex for weapons. Alex said, "Oh I am not here to shoot anyone. Anyways, I don't do it with men. I mean not in brotherhood. Yes, that's about it."

The fat man grumpily gestured another one. He said, "One grand for one kilo. Good enough for you."

Alex waved his hands, "Oh, normally on first deals I give complimentary stuff. But free things don't get their worth of attention. Like earlier this day, two hot chicks asked me out, without me hitting on them. So I passed it over, but that doesn't mean that they were not good. Now take this cocaine. How much worth it is, one grand, or maybe 12k, or 14k can't tell, because it depends on how badly you want it. More badly you want, more it will hit."

The fat man smiled and gestured another one, "You are smart, Azrock told us, you want long business."

Alex played with his fingers, "Oh, come on. Girls are felt best, shorter the relationship is, while relationships are felt best longer the night is, and night is felt best on how good the cocaine is. I mean you take the cocaine, try it and tell us on how long our relationship is going to last."

The fat man nodded and raised two fingers, while other said, "Good, we'll give 12k for each kilo. Pass the bag."

The Chinese inspected the bag thoroughly, while Alex pretended that he was talking with a new client in the meeting room of High Rise. That was what held him together, or long before Alex would've hopped back into the cab. Well to be true, it was also the innocence he was trying to prove held him together. While Alex randomly moved his eyes from one man to another to the abandoned building, the fat man who apparently looked as if he was

Chih Ming Ho, was closely checking out Alex, as if he was hugely impressed.

It was like a boss to boss eyeing. The Chinese men showed a thumbs up to their boss while Alex slowly exhaled. This was easy than hitting girls, and also you don't have to take these men to bed, brotherhood was not that bad an experience. They gave Alex a briefcase filled with cash.

The fat man finally spoke, "Good business is in your blood, make every drop count it."

The Chinese moved out in their cars, while Alex felt little puzzled, was this a fortune cookie. Seriously it had to be. But the fat man was right about one thing, make every blood count it of what one was made of. Alex was made of good pants, easy shirts, easy shoes, and easy blazers. No matter how easy they were, he couldn't loose them to an accusation of murder. Alex felt that half the battle was won. Now between him and the Drug Lord was just a cab ride till Terry's house. Though Alex was blamed to be the drug Lord which he was not, but after this deal he thought he would have been a good drug lord too, and this profession was not bad after all. There was respect and there was lots of brotherhood, not like that of Anna's.

On his way back the butchers were still staring at him and his new briefcase, but this time it didn't made any difference, because Alex actually realized how Mia felt while he always stared at her. This was a Mia moment. Alex was little happy too, to tell Terry that he had made 2k extra profit per kilo. Maybe Terry would give him phone numbers of his female customers like those two earlier the day, as Alex realized getting laid with drug addicts was little easy. But right now, proving his innocence was more important.

The apartment of Terry was empty. Terry was nowhere in the house. Alex searched hard, and found nothing. He asked few neighbors if they had seen Terry, but no one knew. Maybe he must have gone to sell some drugs. Alex waited, for Terry. The clock moved from one to two to three to four hours. It was past midnight, and there was no sign of Terry. Alex crazily thought, where did all his brotherhood go. Staying at Terry's house was not safe especially when Terry was not around, because if Police found him here with this money and more drugs in bedroom, he would be screwed like hell, so he called Nathan to check if they could meet.

Nathan said, "Alex, where have you been, and what are you doing. We are worried, I hope the deal went well."

Alex said, "Hey, all's good. Wait, how did you know about the deal?"

Nathan said, "Of course I know, you are now officially the drug lord. I can't believe it. Just turn on the TV."

Alex found the remote, turned it on, while Nathan said, "Hey Alex, remember we are here. I know you are good at pants, but when it comes to head, you can reach us. Hey Julia is calling, just watch the news."

Nathan hanged the phone. Seriously, Julia was still with him, Alex couldn't believe. But one thing was sure that these girls with dresses of Milan were all stupid without realizing from where the glory of Romans came from, Julius Ceaser fanatic of Cleopatra who herself didn't like dresses of Milan, in fact he didn't even liked dresses, and these girls are influenced by fashion of such places without knowing what the real deal was.

Wait, WTF! Alex increased the volume of TV, and it went like 'One Grand for One Kilo, Good enough for you'. Holy shoot, this was the video of Alex's deal with Chinamen on National TV. What the hell was happening,

Alex thought. He took the pillow of couch and held it tight, not because the video was of good quality or he was making the headlines again, but Prison didn't had pillows which even Alex didn't realized. He murmured where the Brotherhood was gone, that prick ditched him. Maybe he was the same man that ditched Audrey the other day. Why couldn't he see that this deal was also from the same man.

Detective Joe was talking with a journalist saying 'Now we have solid evidence that he is the drug Lord. He is wanted for a murder of two and running illegal drug syndicate'. Wait, murder of two, wasn't maths of Detective wrong. He turned the channel which was showing a footage of Alex's apartment, with a dead body lying on ground. That dead body was of Terry. Alex just felt his feet loosing ground.

A detective explained the reporter that the victim is a drug peddler, Terry who probably would have revolted against Alex and got murdered. He too was killed by a knife, with a deep wound in belly, same fashion as Audrey was killed. We not only suspect but are sure that same person killed them both. The detective turned to camera and said, and it is Alex. Alex if you are watching this, know that we are coming for you.

Alex said to himself, 'I never used the same pose for even different girls, and this detective blamed me for a murder in same fashion. This detective had to be kidding me'.

Alex re-watched the video footage being played on TV. God the CCTV cameras that captured it were too good and charming face of Alex was too visible in it. He never felt being that played, and realized how girls would feel when he tricked them into bed. Life was taking a complete circle for Alex. This was why that dog Terry wanted him to do the deal. Alex panicked, and realized that he must get out from Terry's house before Police raided this place. He took the briefcase of cash, and went straight out to get a cab. The butchers were still staring at him, while he eyed them and thought that this was not over yet. Yes it wasn't over.

Alex wanted to prove himself innocent, while he ended up doing another crime, not the killing of Terry but that drug deal. It was a dream of sleeping with lesbians coming true, as you get the another too. Maybe Anna had cursed him, but really did curses even worked in age of VR make out. Nope. But the question was who killed Terry. Maybe the drug Lord was scared that Terry would spill out his name and expose him, so he killed Terry. This was the closest explanation this murder could have. One thing was sure that Alex was moving in the right direction, though as always there were distractions like the other girls, but this catch, Terry did hit the right spot. Alex kept watching his footage on TV on a new mobile phone Terry had given him. Seriously, it was more humiliating than featuring on a porn. But Alex had to do something. These Policemen's faith was getting stronger. Alex thought for a while and opened the Angelano Police Department website.

He called Joe and said, "Detective, it's me Alex, the white man, White because I am clean. Really all clean."

Joe said, "Oh, oh. Alex it's nice to hear from you. I know if you wash good, even blood stains can go. Now listen boy, surrender yourself. This time we know who you are, and you are not getting out of this. If you'll keep running you might fall, not because of that stone on path, but by a bullet in your back."

Alex said, "Okay just think. If I was the drug lord that Audrey wanted to uncover, why did she came with me to the hotel room that night. A respectable journalist with a smudgy drug lord, think."

Joe said, "Oh we don't doubt your skills. We saw how you sold a 10k stuff in 12k."

Alex said, "Okay, if I was the drug lord, why did I killed Audrey by myself, and not by my men."

Joe said, "Oh probably because you are straight and didn't want another man in hotel room that night."

Alex exclaimed, "Oh no detective. I mean yes I am straight, in fact straightest of them all. But just think. I am a drug lord, and would I want to get in another case of civilian murder."

Joe said, "Okay maybe you made Terry kill her, and then you killed Terry."

Alex snapped back, "But you were sure that same person killed Audrey and Terry both."

Joe said, "Listen I am not a teen punk girl whom you can convince easily to sleep with. Of course I am not sleeping with you. But this wont work, surrender yourself and I might recommend leniency to the Judge."

Alex hung up the phone and felt like screaming. He had reached to the outer Angelano in a highway hotel. He took a room and went straight in. He opened the suitcase of cash and there were 60 thousand dollars. Phew, they were enough to keep him on run and prove his innocence. God, there was lots of money in drugs. I mean, this was the salary of Alex of an entire year that he made in just one meeting. In one meeting, seriously, it was more money than Mia made in her stage shows. It was the virgin money, yeah as Alex had lost his virginity of crime with this deal. But that officer, God, Alex wanted to throw a rotten sneaker on his face. He was not ready to listen anything.

For a minute Alex thought of killing him, and blaming the murder on that Drug Lord that tricked him. But whoa, he was the drug lord now. What a situation it was, he was being blamed of everything he did and everything that Drug Lord did. Alex thought that framing him for two murders wasn't that easy, and some trickster mind must be behind all this. Wait, what if the drug lord had hired some hit man to do the job. Also both the murders were committed in same fashion, meaning probably by same person. It made sense, like every time on hustling night he needed a wing man, this drug lord took help of a hit man and got killed these both. And what if he found that hit man and made him confess that someone told him to kill them both.

Alex picked the phone. As he didn't had his phone book, so searched for Star Line properties, and dialed the number. It was the number of his broker, ahem, the real estate broker of course as our man was not into illegitimate things. His name was Delvin, and he was friends with Alex. He often took tips for hitting women by Alex, and in return got fixed the plumbing, cable TV, and internet connection.

Delvin said, "Alex, my buddy. You are the man. You killed two freaking people, while you always told me that you can't even pick 20 lb box. Man now I think your balls are heavier than 20 lb. Ha ha."

Alex said, "Hey Delvin I appreciate that. But I need help, and you can't tell this to anyone."

Delvin said, "Ah, you doubt that. Did I ever tell Mr. Walter that you nailed her daughter? No because, even I want to nail her. Come on man, just get rid of police then give me some tips to hit on Junior Walter."

Alex interrupted, "Hey I will, I will. But I remember you talking about hiring professionals to scare the tenants, or abandon the property. In short I need a hit man, the best one, if you got any contact."

Delvin knew many shady people, and he gave Alex the number of city's best hit man. By the way Mr. Walter was the same man that stood out of Alex's apartment in short pants. Yes he was the landlord, and had a daughter who had just made into college. She often visited Alex to learn Economics, and one night things got funneled to the basics. Supply - Demand, Supply – Demand, Supply – Demand, and the night went on like that. Alex was really good when it came to Supply – Demand, meaning economics. Now Alex just needed to find what hit man did this work of murder.

~~

Chapter 5

Alex had heard that crime was like chain smoking, once you get into it, there was no stop to it. But it was now he realized that his life was on fire. A detective who was so dumb that he couldn't see that drug lords don't have a first class degree in marketing, nor did they had a day job, nor would they dump a dead body into their own rented apartment, nor would they have posters of playmates in their room. Well the last one could have been offensive to sexuality of criminals, but didn't they all preach brotherhood. Only if Alex would have fantasized about situations like getting tangled in crime instead of legs, it would have been easier now.

Alex had reached the Old Castle Market, which was infamous for illegal sales of arms and weapons, while few knew that it also was home to hit men of the city. It was visiting a second market on second day of run. Alex couldn't have asked more as a marketer, to actually visit such glorifying places that normal people avoided. Of course when life ends there is only glory left, right. From outside the market looked like an antiques market, but then he saw an Arabian carpet getting unfolded to reveal guns within them. He asked to few people around where he could find Lawrence. But nobody helped him.

A man at shop looked at Alex and said, "Isn't he the Audrey Killing case suspect."

The shop owner snapped back, "So what look there, that shop owner, he was once a serial killer. And over there, that faggot looking man has 3 kidnappings to his name. And look at me, yes me, right in front of you, have 2 times robbed the same bank, with same manager on gunpoint of same gun."

The man said, "Got it. Only if Audrey was still alive, would have died to die again in this market."

A small time hawker noted Alex roaming and asking around everybody. He approached Alex and told him the way to Lawrence's office. It was on top floor of a laundry shop. Yeah, cleanest place a hit man could have his headquarter at. He entered and Lawrence's office reminded Alex of High Rise and Christie's condo office. Yes this too had a living room, bedroom, and a toilet attached. But no way that Alex fantasized himself in this place, on that bed.

Lawrence said, "You're Alex right. Come sit, Delvin told me about you. So whom do you wanna sleep."

It sounded strange and Alex said, "Sleep? Well, Mia could be one, but obviously you don't know her as your taste is music is something I can feel. But you can help me with something."

Lawrence made an angry face, and pointed his finger to his assistant who turned on the music. It was, Whatever, Whenever, by Mia, a song from her first album. Both Lawrence and his assistant started doing a strange belly dance which didn't suited there fat belly. But the groove was getting better with music.

Alex said, "Okay okay, you have a good taste in music. Now here is the thing. I am in search of a hit man who probably killed Terry and Audrey."

Lawrence high fived his assistant and said, "Oh so you too are a hit man, coz as I know you killed them."

Alex held his head, "Look, let's just pretend I didn't killed them, do you know anyone who might have."

Lawrence got thinking and tossed a coin to catch it with one hand. Alex pulled 5 thousand dollars from his pocket and placed it on the table. Lawrence smiled and got his assistant bring his phone along with bottle of vodka. He made a drink for Alex, and showed him a WhatsApp group, seriously, a WhatsApp group that had all the Hit men of this city as group member. He pointed to one particular message that said, 'Hey, I am leaving, got some work to do. There is a peddler I need to take care of.'. Alex almost jumped from his seat.

Alex exclaimed and gulped the drink, "Lawrence, don't ask me to sleep with you, or I will. I got this."

He continued, "I need to talk to this man. Please Lawrence help me."

Lawrence had got his money, and he gave Alex a card. It was the hit man calling card. Nope, it didn't had any prepaid balance in it, but a template to fix a meeting with hit men of Angelano. Seriously this industry was on a whole new level, Alex thought. Only if there was a template to hit on women, no shot would go empty. Even a private limited company like High Rise didn't had meeting templates and the people were assumed to type in lengthy charming mails. Lawrence also gave him a rate card, but to hell, Alex didn't need that. He texted the message to Eddie, yes that was the hit man talking about taking care of peddler, and this was just two days back, while Angelano wasn't that big to have that many peddlers to be taken care by a hit man. Finally everything had got back on track. Alex was glad that he called Delvin who literally fixed this. Just a meeting with this hit man, and then a confession.

But wait, Alex thought on why would a hit man confess to his crimes. Damn, why didn't he thought about it earlier. He had 50 thousand dollars more, maybe he would have given this money to hit man for a confession and flee from this city forever, but what if the hit man denied. Alex thought maybe then he will record his confession and send it to the detective. Great, But then Lawrence and these WhatsApp friends would wildly chase Alex for his life. But that could be handled, as Alex was open to moving places, anyways what has this city given to Alex, an accusation of masturbating on a dead body, the grossest of things he can't even imagine.

Alex stayed with Lawrence and waited for the evening, when their meeting was scheduled. Lawrence had told Alex to schedule it in Frankie's bar. It was near, and safe for meeting. Lawrence showed Alex his collection of music, and damn he turned out to be a bigger fan of Mia. He had signed CD's of Mia's music, it was like keeping the lingerie after make out. Alex couldn't believe that Mia was that popular, and also feared that his music CD sales will ever go down and he will never have his chance. The hours went by, and Alex played shooting games on brand new play station Lawrence had. It was evening 6, and Alex left for Frankie's bar with a picture of Eddie in his phone. He got seated in a corner seat, and after waiting for half an hour a man came in hiding badly with a long over coat.

Alex recognized him and said, "Wow so that's you. It has to be you."

Eddie said, "Listen Alex. I am sorry, but it got screwed up. You will need to pay me 25 thousand more and the work will be done. I mean its half done now, but full after the payment."

Alex confusingly said, "Are you crazy, what did you did? Oh, please not that."

Frankie's bar had a television kept in center, and the news started playing. It was Detective Joe Wilson on air, and was looking extremely mad and upset. He held his arms tightly and pulled the camera on his face. Detective said,

'He called me, and threatened me. When I refused to help, as I never have ever helped any criminal or ever will I. So when I refused to help him. He shot me. Yes, he tried to kill me. He tried to kill a federal detective. He attacked the government. He attacked honesty. This man Alex is a highly dangerous man and needs to be taken down. Policemen of Angelano, who are listening this, I have to say, that even if you are not assigned with this case, it is your duty to catch this Alex who is poisoning our society and its girls'.

Alex just lost his head. Yes it appeared that Detective had shot Alex in his head with his words. Alex was now more entangled. Remember the template that Lawrence gave to Alex, was a contract proposal, and hit men of Angelano only responded when they got a proposal. Out of fun, Alex had typed, Detective Joe Wilson as the name, and Ransom as 50 thousand dollars. Yes the lives of policemen was also on sale in this city, and Eddie did what he was best in doing, he tried taking detective down. But the bullet missed and hit Detective's arm. Alex thought thanks god the detective was not dead.

He slowly yelled at Eddie, "Why did you shot him. I just wanted to meet you."

Eddie snapped, "Hey look, I am not a teen girl that goes on date. You gave a proposal and I accepted it."

Alex held his head, "But what about, you don't fulfill the contract unless you are paid."

Eddie said, "Yes, I did it when I received my 50 thousand dollars. So I did it."

Alex surprisingly said, "Wait, somebody gave you that 50 thousand dollars. Can't believe it."

Meanwhile a policemen on patrol had also entered Frankie's bar, and was having a drink, when he noticed these both and the news flashing on TV. His brows took a curve when they both started watching the TV to start a quarrel. He pulled out his gun and pointed at Eddie and Alex, and told them to put their hands in air. For a minute, life appeared dead to Alex, and he did what the Policeman said. The policeman approached their table, and the waiter who had got Alex's order of two frappe also got closer without seeing the policeman. Alex then pushed his foot to Eddie who fell back straight on policeman. Alex ran with all the strength he got. He didn't cared to turn back and look if he was being chased. Today either he would have escaped that policeman or got hit by a bullet on his back. It was do or die for Alex.

After all this, all the fantasies of Joe Detective would come true if he was caught. Alex ran, street after street, turn after turn, block after block, and had gone too far to be caught. Seriously, he had become a seasoned criminal in eyes of Angelano PD. Later Alex saw on mobile that Eddie was caught and he confessed to being given a contract to kill Joe Winslow. Seriously all this day Alex had prayed god for Eddie's confession, and he did, but this was not the way it was supposed to happen.

Nathan called Alex on his new number, "Alex, what the hell you are doing. You tried killing the detective. Is this your version of proving yourself innocent? Do you have any idea how scared we are?"

Alex said, "God, Not now Nathan. Things are screwing up, and I don't wonder why. All my life I have only honed myself for screwing, and here we are. Wait, what are you eating."

Nathan said, "Oh Muffins. I have even planned to cook it for you when you be free of all this."

Alex was still panting, "Didn't I just told you, I am good at screwing. Screw you."

Alex hung up the phone, and sat on a lonely public bench. Alex thought, systematic, my foot that Eddie didn't even checked who gave him those 50 thousand dollars and did the work. God, why only me? If God was there, he totally misunderstood what Alex wanted from him. He had asked for girls behind him, not guns. Yuck, not guns with smell of gunpowder. Everything felt like falling apart. Within three days, he had been accused for a murder of an innocent girl, running a city wide drug syndicate, doing a live drug deal, killing a drug peddler, and hiring a hit man for killing a federal detective. Oh no, the judge was sure going to faint when his case would come up.

These crimes would have only led him to lifetime of imprisonment, or maybe a death penalty. Alex thought to himself, maybe he should surrender, and talk out some sense to the policemen, because if anything else went wrong, he would not be able to cover up things. God, but Police would never listen to him. They will simply shove him into prison. Alex took a cab, and went back to that hotel. Hiding his face he got into the room while someone knocked. Wait, who could be it. Alex slowly went towards the door and tried peeping out from window besides.

He opened the door and said, "Some messes just can't be cleaned."

It was the housekeeping, and he shut back the door. It reminded him of Audrey, though it was against the rules to remember your one night stands, but he did. Audrey what a girl she was, brave, intelligent, and daring. She didn't care who the drug lord was and she hit the road to catch him. He remembered the gun she carried, a girl carrying a gun in a night club. Seriously, if Audrey can do it, why can't Alex, he thought. He made his mind, even if he would lose his life the fight of proving himself innocent was worth it.

He didn't do all of this, but one who did should be scared now. He thought of screaming, but that would attract people on his doorstep, so he did that in his mind. Alex got hold of himself. He knew that this drug lord was two steps ahead of him. That drug lord was watching Alex, and his every move. Now Alex had to be smarter in doing anything, without leaving any traces. Catching this drug lord was only possible if he had some loop holes in his acts, similarly like Alex left them in his acts. If Alex can commit mistakes, then that drug lord must also have committed some, so why not dig them deeper. Alex ran his mind, and there he got it. Eddie had showed Alex a message of receiving 50 thousand dollars. It was transferred to his bank account. Voila, it must have been transferred from some account, and if Alex got to know about that some account, he might find the drug Lord. The tables had turned again, and Alex was back in the mission innocent.

The television was still on, while Alex lay for few seconds of catching breath, before he caught that freaking drug lord. Alex was everywhere, anyone would want to be, on Talk shows, on Prime time news channels, on newspapers, and in all those blah blah blah, but he was only for wrong reasons. His recent journey had caught hold of Mayor and of course the commissioner of Police. They were giving statements about him. As one of them went like this.

The commissioner said, 'Enough the Police of Angelano has been fooled, and our kids drugged, but not anymore. We will bring justice to all the youth of Angelano that didn't deserve drugs. Well anyone as a matter of fact doesn't deserve drugs in the city. We know the man behind it, Alex, and soon he will be standing getting convicted of his crimes in your own court of law.'.

While the Mayor was saying, 'Our Daughters aren't objects to be played and destroyed. They are the humans of Angelano, and if anybody brings harm to them, I swear they will pay for it, even if it were my son. What has happened to our city, men like Alex are roaming free committing crime after crime? People of Angelano we need you now the most. If anyone knows about this womanizer who might be on his way to prey on some other woman, tell us first.'. The city of Angelano has never been that together. Alex thought that it was so funny that a man who always sought hookups had finally hooked up the people of this city together but against him. Lots of damage control was to be done, Alex covered his face with the quilt.

At Angelano Police Department, Joe Wilson was back in action despite of being hit by a bullet on his arms. He was talking to his assistant Leroy who had taken the testimony of Hit man Eddie.

Leroy said, "There is something interesting detective. I just took the statement of Eddie and he told me something you wouldn't believe. As per him, yes he was contacted by Alex to kill you, but later Alex told him that was just to setup the meeting and he didn't wanted to kill the detective, you."

Joe strangely said, "Seriously, placing a contract to meet the hit man. It has to be better than this."

Leroy continued, "What's more strange is that the ransom of your head, 50 thousand dollars were paid to Eddie from some other person and not by Alex, as Alex told him. I checked it, and the money has come from Bank of Bahamas. But as you know we don't have diplomatic ties with Bahamas to extract that information."

Joe said, "This Alex is a hard nut. But you know there is a voice inside me that says it's not Alex."

Leroy said, "To echo that. Alex's GP has confirmed that his blood samples from routine checkups never had drugs."

A policeman came in rushing towards Joe, and he handed him some pictures. It was of Alex, taken just outside the hotel he was staying. Joe looked at them and the policeman told that sender of this picture is anonymous friend of Angelano. Joe got both of them to a corner.

Joe said, "Hey, this is between us. I don't want you to arrest Alex, just keep an eye on him."

Leroy said, "Detective are you convinced that he is not the drug lord or killer."

Joe snapped, "I just said, it's not him. What I think is he might not be alone. There must be a bigger group working behind these acts, while using Alex as a cover face."

They separated while the policeman took another assistant to keep an eye on Alex. This was like trouble getting started for Alex. Not even one person in the city didn't believed that Alex was innocent. The policemen had parked their vehicle just outside the hotel. Alex was laying low on bed, when he remembered his first one night stand. Yeah that was the best thing to occur to his mind, as this night wasn't getting over. That girl was his school mate, and had a crush on Alex, while Alex used to eye the cheerleaders.

On night they made out, Alex had told her, 'Look, this all was good. In fact we can do it again. But in between, there has to be nothing else.'. The girl had told Alex in return that 'There will come a day when nothing for between will be left.'. Alex knew that it was her curse becoming true today. Nothing was left for in between. Conclusions were already made, and the ending was decided.

~~

Chapter 6

The entire night Alex couldn't sleep, thinking about Prison time, the gross food they gave to convicts, and all you could do for satisfaction was read dirty magazines or puff a cigarette. No, this was not acceptable, after all Alex wanted to hit Floor on Fire again, well not really the same club, more like them. This time Alex had a plan, and he already felt like a champ, to lay down later this night with joy of being one step closer to innocence. Well yes, lay down, but not with any girl. Alex was a marketer and being a marketer it was his job to know about all things digital. Yes apart from sexy Anime girls, he knew a thing or two about hacking. This was what was going to save him from disaster.

Alex knew a hacker named Marvin, who once also had hacked him a list of Phone numbers of girls that contested Miss Angelano. Though Alex's crusade of hooking with any one of them had failed, but point was that Marvin was a damn good hacker. Wait, that crusade failed, yes it did, but then Alex thought what has that failure to do with his current plans. Marvin had his computers shop in Witch Field market, and Alex would give him every hacking related work he got in High Rise. Out of that friendship Marvin would definitely help, as Alex thought. The policemen that were keeping an eye on Alex had got Alex's attention. Alex had noticed their car since late night. He knew that it had to be the men of drug lord. But he didn't do a thing, rather just moved out of the hotel room. While on way he saw few hippies hopping into their mini truck. Alex went closer to them and said, "Hey, looks the city is going to get more cool. Headed where?"

The hippie said, "Nah! We are headed back home. City gets cooler when you have bucks."

Alex gave a winning smile, "Anything for coolness of city. I mean here is thousand dollars, only if you hit that car with your truck and make them go round after you in the city."

Hippie grinned, "Okay with us, if you want to see how we get things rolling."

Alex entered their mini truck while the policemen watched, but he also hopped down from other gate of the van, which the Policemen couldn't see. The hippies started the car with a roar, and next was hotel receptionist coming out from his desk hearing a crash noise. The hippies were actually little more rude on policemen and kept hitting till the Policemen started their car to chase back Hippies. The mini truck vroomed into air, while Policemen chased thinking Alex was getting away.

Alex had won in getting rid of men of Drug Lord as he assumed, but he didn't knew what he had just done. He took his belongings and got off the hotel. His next stop was Witch field market. It was the biggest computer market in city, where you could get just about everything, and Alex knew every corner of it. In last few days, it was the third market he was visiting, and hoped that this time he got what he sought. Alex went from lane to lane, hiding his face, searching for Marvin's shop. For a minute he realized whether Marvin's shop had moved, but it was only the confusing lanes of market.

Alex was also watchful if somebody was following him. Few of peddlers did, but he knew they just meant to sell those dirty DVD's. Well, it has been long he has watched that kind of stuff, but time wasn't right. One dirty night had already created lot of trouble, now if he was caught with those DVD's, who knew if Detective Joe Winslow also accused him of running illegal porn industry in the city. Well actually this accusation would have been the best of all that actually Alex had enjoyed doing in real. But clearly he wasn't part of any of them. He finally found Marvin's shop where Marvin's boys were selling Mac books black marketed from China. Alex eyed Marvin, and they both went inside the room behind Marvin's shop where he had all his hacking tools and kits.

Marvin said, "Dude, you are in deep trouble. I just can't stop watching you on TV."

Alex sighed, "Yeah I have been told worse, on how deep this trouble is. But listen I need some help from you, and you just can't tell anyone about it."

Marvin nodded and said, "Did you really masturbated on a dead body. It's hard to accept."

Alex snapped, "Hey I might score low on women. But can't be that low. Now let's get to work."

Alex still had Eddie's number and even the message that doomed him. He got Marvin note that number, and asked him to hack the Mobile phone network and get details of all messages transacted on Eddie's number. It was a tough task, but not for Marvin who was a champ at this. In fact he had pre built software to hack into such big companies.

Marvin clicked few times and said, "Here are the messages. Hey is that of a girl, cause this is not the best time when entire city police is after you."

Alex closely looked at all the messages. The last one was about meeting point at Frankie's bar. The messages went on like, 'Hey tonight hit my place, I am wearing your favorite red down under'. For a minute Alex thought of noting that number down, as this girl liked a hit man, and why wouldn't she sleep with the drug lord of the city, but then the time wasn't right. Another message read, 'Hey, did you deposited the school of fees. Dan has been warned of it'. Seriously this red undie lover was a dad too. Woah, Alex had just destroyed the future of Dan who would not be able to attend school because his dad was arrested now. Alex felt the guilt, and moved on. Another message was sent by Eddie, 'Hey you, I will sue you and your Chinese Food truck. You sell dog's meat in hot dogs. Peddlers in my village do better than this you freak'.

Wait, this was the peddler Eddie was talking about in that WhatsApp group. Oh shoot, how didn't he realize that it could also be a food peddler. But seriously, Dog's meat in Hot Dog was crazy. He moved on, and this was the message he had been looking for, '50,000 credited to your account number ABN8009610 Bank of Bahamas'. Alex pointed the message to Marvin, and smiled wickedly.

Marvin burped, "Alex, do you want me to hack into his bank. Really?"

Alex nodded while Marvin said, "Dude, officially you are the drug lord, and what do you want me to become, a bank robber, cause I think that will justify our friendship."

Alex said, "Come on Marvin you can do it. All you have to care of is staying off the radar, and we will be friends like a good marketer is to a good hacker."

Marvin started tickling his fingers. It was the Bank of Angelano where Eddie had his account. They had recently got a new cyber security system in place as per newspapers. It took some time, but Marvin successfully hacked into the internal web network of the bank, but what was required was logging into that system using an employee ID, and it was where they got stuck. It was highly secured Login system where network could get blocked if someone entered wrong Login credentials for continuous three times. Marvin showed him the screen and explained the dead end.

Alex felt exhausted, "There has to be some way Marvin, but please don't tell me to get Employee ID credentials. I can't walk into that bank, especially with Police Headquarters beside it."

Alex started walking out from room when Marvin snapped back. "Wait, there is another way. If we create a fake bank ATM panel, and try to access Eddie's account from it. It might allow us in with all his last 30 days transaction. But that will need some money. Fake ATM Panels are available on dark net, but starts from least 5 thousand dollars, and there is no guarantee to it. It could also raise an alarm with police at our doorstep in next 30 minutes."

Alex opened his briefcase with money falling from it, and Marvin clicked on buying the ATM panel. They strode out into the nearest Starbucks for Public Wi fi and Marvin got his Laptop to work.

Marvin said, "The account sender of those 50 thousand is MH9332456LP from Bank of Bahamas."

Alex thumped his fists into Marvin's, "That's great now find me the account holders name of this account."

Marvin frowned, "This will not be easy, and a federal crime it will be. See we don't have diplomatic ties with Bank of Bahamas, and if we are found trespassing their bank, we could even start a war, and be blamed with anti-national intent of disturbing the national security. Dude this is bigger than being a drug lord. Do you still want me to?"

Alex said, "Really, a crime more grave than being a drug lord."

Marvin said, "You know its like hooking up with your girlfriend's sister."

Alex snapped back, "But I don't make girlfriends, so it will be like hooking up with two sisters."

Marvin made a disappointing face, "I know that, you know that, but Angelano PD. Hmm?"

The last thing Alex wanted now was being accused of another crime. Wait this was serious business Marvin was talking about. Maybe tomorrow's headline would run like, Wanted, Terrorist Alex, and ransom two pair of lingerie. Wait no, not pair of lingerie, but pair of millions. Why did these filthy piece of clothing dominated his mind, Alex thought. Now, it was do or die.

The options were simple, to take risk of starting a war and closing this one, or take no risk and die in prison by losing this war of innocence. Damn, why always me God, Alex thought. This was probably Alex's only lead of catching the Drug Lord. He had made a mistake, and it was not necessary he would keep making those mistakes again and again. Alex saw a policeman entering the Starbucks. Damn it, Alex thought, no way I am going to die in prison after being arrested by a pimple faced virgin. Life can't just F me.

Alex turned, "Its war then."

Marvin pulled his hoodie on and got plugged into his laptop. Bank of Bahamas was a triple layered security system, but there was a loophole in it. Every three hours, a security program ran to do audit of the entire software system. At that time the triple layered security always made an exception for that security program. Now what Marvin had to do was corrupt that security program and enter inside the Bank of Bahamas mainframe along with the program and fetch all the information required.

The bad news was that this security program also got scanned every time it entered the mainframe. The good news was that Marvin was one of the hackers that were contracted to test the code structure of a similar security program. So Marvin knew about these security programs, and how it was built. In minutes he was into the Bermuda Info Com server inserting his code into the security program. Now both waited to see it that worked. It was only 10 minutes before the audit would start. They drank coffee, and never had wished for climax to come earlier than expected, especially Alex, never.

Marvin said, "Do you know, you are the drug lord. And for the integrity of this title shouldn't we also rob a couple of millions from Bank of Bahamas, and then flee to live in some of their beaches never to be caught."

Alex grinned, "Hey, that's all cool, but then who will supply drugs in the city. Imagine, sex rates of first meet up falling in the city. Of all things, I can't be part of such a crime."

Marvin popped, "Hey we are into their mainframe. Check this out."

The sever of Bank of Bahamas was hacked and it was fetching all similar bank accounts. They spotted the one they were looking for. Alex had pen and paper ready, but then he thought what the F was this in digital age, of course Marvin would be able to copy those details. There it was, the bank account number MH9332456LP belonged to a shipping company, First Freight Pvt. Ltd. The account had whooping 11 million dollars. This had to be of the drug lord, who else could make such deal of money, Alex thought. Seriously, with all this money he could buy drinks to all girls of Bahamas, but no more crime, as the deal was. Both moved out back to the shop.

Marvin said, "So, what are you going to do now. This one looks like a huge company. You know such import export companies usually have cut throat lawyers. It would be hard proving something against them."

Both were looking at the website of the First Freight. It was intricate, and better than each of micro websites that High Rise made. Seriously these drug people were game apart. Alex took the laptop and started browsing the site. It had no clear information about the owners of the company, neither did the internet had any such details. As per Marvin, this must have been a new company, with lots of illegal money behind its foundation. But there it was, another lead, a regional office in the city of Angelano.

Alex smiled, and Marvin asked, "Hey hacking is okay, as its easy to go in and easy to come out, like all your hookups. But just think before doing anything. You don't know what might happen, or what might be waiting for you, as these people are no good. Just an advise."

Alex said, "In past three days, I have done a drug deal and made a hit man shoot a federal detective. What makes you think, I am not going to take my chances. Ha".

Well in drugs, there was lot of money as Alex had seen, but not after all they were as glitzy as a fraction of High Rise. This regional office had the address of the port where they had rented a chamber kind of thing. This night Alex went to see if he could find somebody at the office, maybe bribe him with Terry's money, and get some information out. At the port entrance, he didn't expect that much of security. He tried turning around but saw the port being fenced from all sides with huge walls and barbed wire, probably with electricity running thru them. Ah, this looked trappier than his own situation. There was no time to plan to infringe this security, so he moved to the check post.

Alex said, "Hey, I am accountant of First Freight. Need to run some numbers."

The guard said, "Sure sir, but we don't see any appointments for First Freight. Plus it is closed now."

Alex said, "Of course it is, and do you know that the business is drowning in troubled waters of recession. Soon all these offices will be closed and you will have no body to check appointments for. Wait".

Alex took out his phone while panicked guard said, "Its okay sir, please find your way."

This one worked like a charm. Alex knew that Blue collared people feared most of their jobs, only if a person knew how to touch their chords. Sometimes Alex thought that men were fooler than women. Seriously, convincing a woman to a bed is far more difficult than convincing this guard, of course not to the bed. But really. Half of the work was done. Good news was, that Alex was inside the port area, but the bad news was that First Freight office was closed as guard told him. There had to be someway Alex thought. He went across containers to containers, and chambers to chambers, to spot the office of FF. There were two F's, Alex thought, and wished neither one of them was for him. The chamber had a huge lock on its door. Alex looked around and saw few couple of people walking but watching some other way. He took the chance, broke the door, and went inside.

Alex said to himself, "God damn, another crime, trespassing, but not that grave it is."

Alex knew that this office belonged to the drug Lord. Maybe if he could find some drugs inside his office, he would be able to prove himself innocent by connecting the owner of this company to drugs. He remembered the dead body of Audrey, closed his eyes for few seconds and started searching the chamber. But there were only heap of files, and no packets of drugs in here. There was a computer, but was as good as empty as it only had few invoices, and some porn. Seriously, Porn, what was this place, handled by some teenager, well who knew.

Alex's heart was beating as he didn't wanted anybody to enter the room and catch him with another crime. There had to something that could lead him to that drug lord. Alex even tested the water from container kept inside, suspecting if they dealt in some liquid drug. After waiting for ten minutes, nothing happened and he moved on to juggle the entire place. He then spotted a CCTV camera. Wait, am I being watched, he panicked and covered his face from a file. He went near to the camera to see if it was on. Yes it was. Shit, the drug lord must know he was here. He started to leave the chamber. But then turned around, to see it had wire leading to some box, recording everything. He opened it and connected it to the computer. He saw recordings of last seven days, but the office was closed in all recordings, except for once that a man entered and took away few files. Alex felt he had reached a dead end. Maybe these drug people were smarter.

Alex said to himself, "I hate to say this, but Audrey why did you agreed to sleep with me."

He opened his eyes and saw a photograph hanging in chambers along with a certificate from Business council of Angelano. There were three people in the photograph, and one of them was Jody Bradley. Guess who was it? None other than the commissioner of Police himself, Shit!

~~

Chapter 7

Police was corrupt, Audrey had told him, but the commissioner of Police too was part of this drug racket. Alex couldn't believe, and thought that he would never get justice, nor will Audrey. Now whom should he look upon, if the Police was of no help. Who knew that even Detective Joe Winslow could be a part of this drug racket. What the F this was. Was Audrey killed by commissioner of Police, oh no, oh no, oh no, Alex held his head. It all made sense, on why Police was coming to conclusions so early, on why did they didn't even talked with Alex before blaming him with all the charges. Seriously, Alex thought, he had never nailed any daughter of Police officer, so why did this was happening to him. In fact he respected daughters of Policemen. He had refused to sleep with one of the girls of police officer, telling her that he can't become the convict of her love. Of all that honesty, this was what Alex was getting.

The doors were closing for Alex to prove his innocence, while this commissioner of Police was giving statements on National TV about him being a creep. Seriously, if while making out a girl screams, that doesn't means she is asking for help. Well the question was now who would help Alex. Alex couldn't have told this to anyone, as either no one would believe, or even if anybody did, the police will come after him with all force for accusing their boss. It all made sense, that how Terry got sold, how Eddie got screwed, only a policeman had hands that deep to hit the right spot.

Well, Alex looked around and thought, that maybe he should find some more evidences.

He took out a file case with 'Containers on Board' heading, and started reading the papers. They had information about all the containers present currently in port. What if some of these containers had drugs? He could at least call the media, and expose this son of a gun. Yeah that sounded well. He went up to one of the containers to only find that it was locked. Alex had read somewhere that port people had access to all the containers, so he needed to find a port ground staff. He clicked some pictures and went back towards gate.

Alex said, "Hey I need you to open a container for me. I need to check if goods are all right."

The guard hesitatingly said, "But sir, only the shipping company supervisor can make me do that."

Alex said, "You know what, this consignment can wait, as this is the last one. You might have not heard, but Angelano traders are being boycotted. Not a problem. Anyways First Freight is going down. As their accountant, I have made arrangements to declare their bankruptcy, and get rid of the rent for these containers in port. Let it rot."

The guard gulped, "Sir, it would not be needed. Please follow me."

The guard again got a little emotional about his job and the profits of port. Blue collared men were such soft targets. Alex thought seriously, after all this was over, maybe Alex should start hitting on blue collared women. They would be easy to get into bed in minutes. Yeah, blue is so cool. Alex went with the Guard towards container while Guard opened it and got headed back to gate. The container was almost empty with few empty sacks scattered around, and few empty boxes too.

Alex searched them and found white powder in all of them. He tasted the powder. Tingling it was. Damn it that was cocaine. Alex had foreseen it, and there it was. But not enough to call media, to fully expose the commissioner as these empty sacks were covering his half naked body. But one thing was sure that commissioner was the drug lord, or a very close person to the drug lord, and all the trouble Alex was in, was probably designed by this Boss of Policemen. Alex took the pictures of container, and even the cocaine spread in sacks. Coming to the port has been deal of the day. Alex went back to another hotel, and this time he made sure that he wasn't seen. The new hotel was in the old busy district of city where he would be least expected.

Alex called Nathan. "Alex, how are you. You know it hurts me every time I think of you being on run."

Alex said, "This sprint is becoming like a marathon. Anyways, listen Nathan, I have found something. Heard of Jody Bradley, the commissioner of Police? I think he is the drug lord, or part of this syndicate for sure."

Nathan said, "Whoa! This must be the worst news I have heard about lately. Listen Alex, I don't know what people are behind it. But as you say, I am little concerned. See he is the Commissioner of Police. So, be careful. You will need, lots of evidences against him. But just don't get into any trouble."

Nathan continued, "By the way, I am eating a pepperoni pizza now, your favorite."

Alex smiled, "Please don't name it. Damn, I can't even walk into the Domino's."

Nathan said, "Don't worry Alex. Once this is all over, I and Julia will make the best Pizza you ever had that too homemade. We have been practicing a lot. Julia is saying hi."

Alex felt like firing a gun shot right from the phone, and he hung up. Seriously, now after Muffins, it was making Pizzas. This Julia was getting all Italian with Nathan, but when it came to him all she had was an Indian Namaste. What the hell was wrong with Julia? Was she also importing undies from Italian Milan, after all those dresses. Alex thought, when this all will be over, the first thing he would do is take a vacation in Italy and learn all their cuisines. And then it will be just, him, Julia, and that smudgy pasta in between them. But then Nathan was right, Commissioner of Police was a hard nut to crack, and bringing him down would need more evidences. That traces of cocaine in container, was like possessing a small dose of drugs for personal use with a convict charge of community service. This would do no good. He had to be smarter, Alex thought. The best bet Alex could place was keeping an eye on Commissioner and find evidences against him, or probably make him confess about his crimes.

Alex knew that all of this was going to be hard, but he had to start from somewhere. What could be the best place to find out more about the commissioner? He was top policeman and would know where to keep his secrets safe. In fact he would know how to think like a criminal. But Alex didn't wanted to think like a criminal. Because it was like thinking like a woman before hitting on one, and never get laid. But then sometimes you just don't want to get laid. So it has to be the criminal way. Alex had already broken into First Freight office and their container. Now the next target was Jody's office. Yep, if Jody was an organized man, he would definitely be keeping his secrets safe in there.

The office of Police Commissioner was someplace, where Jody would least suspect anyone breaking in. If only Alex found some connection of Jody with drug syndicate, this crusade would become easy. He disguised himself in a long overcoat with high neck collars, tough boots, and entered police building. It was working, no body was noticing Alex. After all, the last thing Policeman would expect is a most wanted criminal walking into their den. Alex even saluted and said hi hellos to few policemen. Jody's office was on top floor. He took the lift and got headed towards it.

A policeman noticed Alex and said, "Hey aren't you Alex, the suspected drug lord and killer of Audrey."

Alex panicked and said, "Yeah you got that right. And now here I am, arrested for my crimes. See you later, as Detective Joe Winslow is waiting for me for interrogation."

Policeman bought it and said, "Think I missed watching the news, and say hi to Joe."

Alex took a deep breath, and that was really pretty close. Alex fastened his steps towards Jody's office. Before coming to Police Headquarters, Alex had called the assistant of Jody and asked her about his schedule, presenting himself to be a journalist who wanted to interview Jody. As per the schedule, Jody was on a field trip between 2 and 5, and it was 2:30, the perfect time to break in to Jody's office. The office was clean, tidy and most importantly empty.

Alex thought, where he should start from. He juggled his desk and found nothing but pending crime charge sheets. He opened his computer, and on desktop the wallpaper was of Angelano's own porn Star, Michelle Sanders. Seriously, this commissioner had lots of trouble in his pants. It was the dirtiest wallpaper Alex had seen, Michelle was licking an iron rod held by a policeman. God, Alex thought that he wouldn't be surprised if that traces of semen on bed sheet were not of Police Commissioner. He searched further, and saw a proposal of putting bounty on Alex's head. Alex threw that file into the Shredder. That was where it should belong. He searched his bag, and found few empty packets. Were they of drugs, Alex thought! Maybe some samples that Jody would give to his customers. Well now as they were empty, they were of no use. He spotted a locker and searched it to find it was stuffed with bras. God, this Jody was a pervert. Well not Pervert, but sick. Well not sick, but just strange. No, Alex didn't had a change of heart, but it reminded him of his bestie from Buffalo who would buy bras and fantasize by wrapping them around pillows. Alex searched further. There has to be something, this Jody is hiding.

Alex then found a briefcase hiding below Jody's desk. It was closed so Alex broke the lock. It had some trade papers. It appeared someone was paying him 100 grand for a consignment. The contract papers were for First Freight, with signature of Jody. It didn't indicated much, but his association with First Freight, which was enough for now. Plus any normal man would know, for what thing someone would pay him 100 grand, nothing but drugs. But the sad part was that Angelano had shortage of normal man, or Alex wouldn't be on run. He took pictures of the paper.

Alex said to himself, "These 100 grand will be your grand entry into Angelano prison."

Alex was furious, sitting in his hotel room. This Jody was making 100 grand in a deal, stuffing his pockets so he could send his daughter to exotic universities so she could have rich foreign boyfriends, while Alex was on run. This was killing Alex from inside. Alex had made his mind to bring down this Jody. No one could get away with murder of Audrey, and murder of Terry, and attempted murder of Joe. But Alex knew that he needed more evidences, more solid evidences. But before all of that it was necessary to confront Jody and let him know that Alex was on him. Was that right. Of course it was. This way Jody would get panicked, and might make some mistakes, or even confess to his crimes without knowing that it could be used against him. But it could also alert Jody that he was being tracked down. Who knew if the Angelano police blamed him of something else, maybe human trafficking or worse being an asset to Terrorist organizations!

Seriously people who can blame Alex for masturbating on a dead body, could do anything, literally anything. Alex thought, only if he could bust Jody with drugs, his case could become strong. But why would Jody pose with Drugs, cocaine. I mean he would prefer those bras, seriously, those were the most plus sized bras, Alex had ever seen. He suspected, if they were of his receptionist, whom Alex had seen and realized she definitely got some silicon injected. Whatever she had done, Alex took his phone out.

Alex texted, "I know about your drugs empire, and First Freight. Count your days you cunt."

Within a minute Jody responded back, "Hey, who is this. Do you know whom you are speaking to."

Alex texted, "A pervert who sleeps with his oversized Receptionist. But now your game is done."

Jody texted back, "Hey, hey hey. What do you want? I can give you money, more than you ever thought of making. Just keep this between us. I think we should meet. Where are you?"

Alex disabled the message reception on his phone, so Jody could know he could receive no more messages. Alex took a deep breath. Well, this did work out. Jody sounded scared, and one thing was sure that Alex had the right man this time, and there was no screwing up. Everything was against him. Alex smiled fantasizing Jody hand cuffed, been taken into custody while Alex gave statement on National TV that criminal has been caught. Yes, that is what would look good on National TV, enough people had hated Alex. Audrey would get her justice, and Alex would find hotter chicks than ever before by being a hero of the city. Alex couldn't stop smiling to day when girls would line up for an autograph, and he would sign them off on their breast.

Alex thought, it's okay god, for doing this all to me. But the war wasn't over yet. Alex had to make his next move, before Jody covered up for his crimes, including sleeping with his receptionist, seriously with that sick fat body, Jody was so gross. Alex ran his mind, where he could get his next evidence. Maybe Jody had a secret apartment where he kept all his illegal trade documents, or maybe a bank locker where he had all his black stash, or maybe in that Receptionist house. No, not in receptionist's house, there Alex would find only oversized bras, that was out. Alex thought, what if Jody's house had secrets no one knew. But that was too dangerous, breaking into Commissioners house. But then where a man keeps his secrets, obviously where he stayed most, that would be his house. The house it is, Alex thought.

Alex waited outside Jody's house, till he got out of house. He had to, because tonight Alex had to break in. There were vehicles coming in and going out, but Jody was still in. For a minute Alex thought, that Jody would not leave this evening, this night. But it was similar to hitting girls, where you always hoped she didn't already had a boyfriend. Wait, she didn't had a boyfriend, No, he had a boyfriend, ah, Jody had a girlfriend, none of that mattered, the point was that Jody in his car was leaving the house. The time had came, only thing between Alex and more evidences was this house. Alex left his car with a paper file, walked towards the house to be stopped by watchman.

Alex said, "Hey easy, I just need to drop this file in Mr Jody's study, and return back with another one."

Watchman said, "Never seen you before, where do you come from."

Alex snapped back, "From Angelano PD, and even I haven't seen you before, are you new here."

It worked, the watchman indeed was new. But this was not a bluff that Alex played. Every watchman services org. did rotation of guards every two to three months, and so this watchman too had to be new. Alex walked inside like a champ. The house was extravagantly big, and obviously smelled of illegal money of Jody. Alex thought seriously, these policemen can notice traces of sperm on a bed sheet, but can't notice that how on a payroll of 100K a govt. servant can get a house made that big. Seriously, what was wrong with people. Alex moved in, and a servant guided him to Jody's study. It was in back of house, and he had to pass through a hallway. Incidentally tonight the hallway was full. It were probably close family members of Jody that had dropped by. Shit! Now how to pass through all these people, Alex thought. These people looked well off, and ones that would watch News every night, implying that they must have seen Alex on National TV. There was no escaping, if Alex got caught here, and who knew if some of these family member were policemen. He opened the file and started reading it while walking aside the hallway. Jody's wife noticed him and stopped Alex.

She said, "Hey, hey. I've seen you somewhere. Are you handling the Audrey murder case?"

Alex panicked, "Uh, yeah, I mean no. I am Audrey's brother. Ah, can't believe she is gone. You must have seen me on TV, they have played my crying video many times. Can't help she was the sweetest sister anyone could get. You know I didn't love her, I mean love is something very small to describe that feeling. I wish, she had not gone to that hotel room that night. Anyways, I was here to drop this file in Mr. Jody's study, and take some paperwork back. I think it will help the police in finding the criminals behind it."

She calmed Alex's cheeks, "Oh, Alex it is. I mean the criminal behind it. He will be caught, don't worry, Jody is the best. Well and the study is that way."

Alex wiped his eyes, though it didn't had tears, but the move always worked with older women. Even if you are wishing to sleep with them, just before you propose, wipe your eyes, it always worked. Well Alex thought, if Jody had such a beautiful wife, why in the world he was screwing his receptionist. Phew, Jody is the Best, Alex chuckled, my foot the best, he kept oversized bras in his locker, instead of some national security level data. Imagine if he became the president of country, he would hoist bras instead of flags. Piece of shit, he was, a corrupt man.

Alex entered Jody's study, which was a huge timbered room. He instantly started juggling the place in hopes of finding something related to Drug syndicate. There were files, files, and files. It appeared that this Jody screwed his receptionist in day, and worked on city crime cases in night in his study. Alex even found his own criminal case file. There had to be nothing in it, but still Alex opened it. All those blamed crimes were there, and then after the last page, voila, there were pictures of Audrey, in bikini, in lingerie, in two pieces, in sexy skirts. Alex felt taken back and for a minute felt offended as if he was really brother of Audrey. This Jody was sick. Alex would easily believe if someone now told him that traces of sperm on bed sheet were of Jody. He took pictures of Audrey and searched further. There was no sign of First freight in his house, literally none. But he found some more empty packets. This time Alex was sure that they were of drugs, but still he couldn't prove it, unless he filled them with drugs and called the DEA to Jody's house. But no, he searched further. Then he found an album of pictures. He took it and turned pages. Voila, oh shoot, oh yes, it was like hitting the jackpot.

The album had a picture of Jody, with guess who. It was with Chih Ming Ho. The same Drug dealer with whom Alex did the drug deal with. Alex could never forget that fat man, and this was it. This picture could clearly prove that Jody had connections with drug dealers of the city.

~~

Chapter 8

Jody was such a rascal. That video of Alex dealing drugs with Chinamen had gone viral on National TV, but Alex never heard the news of those Chinamen getting arrested. Why would they be arrested, after all they were friends of Jody. Now Alex had two evidences against the Commissioner of Police, One that registration certificate of First Freight with clear names of one of director being Jody, and the other a picture of Jody with a Chinese Drug Lord. Alex crushed the face of Commissioner in his mind, thinking he would dearly miss oversized bras in federal prison. Alex thanked god, for doing this to him, he meant not screwing up this time.

For a minute Alex thought that this was enough to bring Jody down, but then his inner voice said. If this is bang-bang then better be more of bangs. Alex thought two evidences were good, but three were better. As when a federal investigation will open against Jody, Alex would not be able to play the prosecutor, but his evidences could do the damage, so why not hit the number three. Not for a minute, pretty face of Jody's wife came to his head who would cry over Jody going to jail. Well actually her pretty face did came to Alex's head, but morphed with a body of 20 something girl in a loud club after all this was over. Yeah, she was pretty. After everything, girls like Audrey will now feel safe in hitting clubs and going to hotel rooms with boys like Alex. This was social good sort of thing.

As Alex had dug, there was a huge party Jody was hosting the other night. Well parties were all same, good food, good wine, good jokes, lots of pictures, and tons of talks. In mid of all this what if Jody met with his crime partners, or had called them in the party. This was a perfect time to catch him with all sinister. Alex got himself made an ID of a local tabloid, with designation of a photographer. He was going to hit the party as a photo man. The plan was good and the night had came. Alex was walking with a newly purchased camera from Terry's blood money.

Alex told the security of party, "Easy with the camera, I have a man to capture."

Alex couldn't help but notice that it was a damn good party. Wife of Jody was personally greeting every guest, while Alex somehow managed to escape her eyes, by lowering his cap towards his face. Everybody was busy chatting and tasting starters. Wait there it was, the enemy of his life, the pain of his heart, reason of his failures, Muffins. Only if Alex had known or was interested in making muffins, that night he would be at Julia's house undressing clothes from Milan and not be lying next to a dead body in a hotel room. Wait, what was that, Alex thought.

I am the star light, to shine in your life,

There is no knife, that can cut us apart,

You and me, me and you, is all what is our life.

Mia, oh freaking god! It was Mia performing this night at the party of Jody. Well, no she was not freaking, in fact she was wearing a shiny blue dress, and looked like an alien who didn't knew anything about sex but yet looked sexiest. Freaking was Jody, who called the pious Mia to his party. What a shame of talent it was, Alex thought. If one would come down to singing at private parties of drug lords, there could be nothing worse. For a second Alex thought, if Mia was staring at him, but then she had her eyes rolling all over the place. Seriously, was singing industry that bad, or this Jody was too rich. Alex thanked god that Mia didn't wore those oversized bras. Wait, what, no way, Mia would entertain Jody, though she was, but only as a singer, not as a person. Alex prayed to god that this all ended soon and Alex could become the hero of her life, and save her from these cheap parties.

In seconds the audience started clapping, of course Mia was good, but wait this was not for Mia, but for Jody that had just entered the party grounds. By the way, this party was hosted on occasion of Jody completing his 25th wedding anniversary. The party got started rolling, and Alex had complete eyes on Jody who was meeting people one by one.

A guest said to passing Jody, "Hey Jody, this wine is so good. Is there drugs in it. Ha."

Jody turned back, "Oh, you just busted the secret of people admiring my food. See ya around."

Seriously, what was that, is there some drugs in it. It was like Alex asking a girl before getting together on bed that hey are you on your periods. What was wrong with people, and what was this party, a drug syndicate get together. Alex thought to himself, Jody crack as many jokes as you can, because these good times are going to end soon. Alex took the tail of Jody and kept following him to bump into a lady almost crushing her breasts.

The lady said, "Hey I know you? What a pleasant surprise, but I didn't saw you on the guest list."

Alex panicked, "Oh, Mrs. Bradley. The pleasure is all mine, for bumping into you. I mean of course meeting you. And apart from being Audrey's brother, I am also a photographer. You know, being Audrey's brother doesn't pays the bill. Phew! She always liked parties, Audrey. In fact we met at a party, I mean she was so busy always, that often we used to meet at parties, me taking pictures, and she wandering around like you. Wish she was here. By the way, you have done an amazing arrangement. This party is lit. So see you around Mrs. Bradley, I have people to capture."

Jody's wife smiled, "Keep bumping into people, this is where you will find happiness. Take care kid."

Take care kid, seriously, Alex thought if he looked like a kid. In fact if a picture was to be taken with Mrs. Bradley and Alex, they would look good couple. Not because Alex was similarly old looking, absolutely not, but Alex always looked good with pretty girls, wait no, there has to Photoshop in that with morphed body of 20 something. Alex murmured, Keep bumping, what else did she think Alex was good at. But seriously those breasts were good, and very deceiving. Now Alex knew, why this Jody had oversized bras in his locker, obviously the seed was planted in backyard.

Alex noticed, that Jody was now meeting with a Chinese man, and it appeared that this Chinese man was some sort of Chief Guest to the party. Jody was literally pampering this sturdy Chinese man. They were talking mouth to ears, and Alex took a picture of them. Wait, this Chinese man looked exactly similar to Chih Ming Ho. Well all Chinese men looked the same, but this one was looking intriguingly similar. Maybe he was the brother of Chih Ming Ho. It has to be as Alex had firm faith on DNA and resemblance. He took more pictures of them, and got closer to listen their conversation and record it as evidence.

Jody said, "Here is to our long friendship. You know even I have been using some of the stuff. Its damn good."

Chinese man grinned, "I know, my teenage is full of stories I made using this stuff."

Jody got excited, "Even a sniff of it, and I feel like I am Hercules. Yeah. You know, it can turn your world upside down. Ah forget this, I have something important to tell you. I have great plans for our stuff, and soon every youth of Angelano will have a packet of it in their pockets. That's my vision. Cheers!".

Seriously, who the hell made this man the Commissioner of Police? This was the sickest thinking a Commissioner could have, a packet of drugs in every pocket. Gross as shit it was. Soon this Jody will get to know, whom he had messed with. After a long, Alex felt his heart to be heavy for Audrey, the poor girl who knew that Police was involved and got killed. That poor soul couldn't even complete a night out with a handsome boy like Alex. I mean in any case what could be a better last night for girl. But damn these people even took that share of happiness for her. Tonight again Alex felt like brother of Audrey. Wait, no, no brother, a well-wisher was just okay.

Coming back to party, the work was almost done, only if Alex could get couple of more evidences. Meanwhile a phone call came and Jody went inside the house talking to somebody. Alex couldn't follow him inside the house, or Jody would recognize his face. So Alex waited outside. Meanwhile Mia had also started doing little moves along with her singing. Seriously this singer, dances too at private parties. Maybe Alex shouldn't wait for all this to get over, and use some of Terry's blood money to hire Mia for private party and save her from such public disasters. But that was too risky, seriously.

Alex sat on a nearby chair and kept watching Mia. God has been so unfair to other girls, by giving such damn good booty to Mia, such a pleasant voice, and a pretty face. In fact, it was such heights of injustice that girls of Angelano should come together and boycott Mia. Maybe then Alex would emerge as a hero and save Mia from disaster. But wait, one side Mia, and on other side all girls of Angelano, oh that was not a good standoff. Jody emerged back from his house. He looked worried, and was sweating in winters, while Chinese man and Alex both approached nearer to him.

Chinese Man said, "Hey is everything all right Jody? Come, my secretary will get you a cock tail maybe. Ha."

Jody wiped his face, "Hey, there is a little trouble. A teenager took our stuff earlier this day, and has gone critical. He is now in hospital, struggling with his life. I think he took an overdose. If this thing gets out, we are finished. God damn, my millions will drown. Do something man."

Chinese man patted on his back, "Easy Jody. You know what business we are into. It happens all the time. I will send some of my men to take care of it. Hey Liling, get him some drinks."

Got you Jody, you are done now, Alex murmured. This was all recorded, and anybody who would listen this will not be hard to convince. By the way, these drug people had all the joy of lives. Seriously, this Liling was a pretty Chinese girl who was now making Jody sip a messy cocktail with her hands. Wait, where was Mrs. Bradley by the way, maybe it was time that Alex called her and start a domestic dispute. Time was going right for Alex so he spotted Mrs. Bradley and told her that Jody was calling him. She went for it and found Liling sitting on Jody's lap.

There it was, the start of troubles for Jody. Ah the work was done, Alex thought, and maybe he should too enjoy the party little bit and especially have some good food after a long feed of room service. Well the seafood was really good, especially prawns. Alex thought maybe Jody had got some drugs added to it, as he had said about the secret, but anyways Alex kept eating them, and most importantly watched Mia perform live.

Seriously life couldn't have been better than being the most wanted Drug Lord of city eating dinner at a party hosted by Police Commissioner, and listening to city's top sensation Mia. What else could one ask for, leaving aside Jody who would say oversized bras, leaving aside Julia who would say muffins or dresses from Milan, leaving aside Christie who would say give me back my soaps, and leaving aside almost everybody in Angelano who wanted something or other. Well the night was done, so was the work of Alex and he was back in hotel.

Now Alex was thinking, maybe he should give these evidences to DEA, or FBI, or maybe both. But there was one thing that bothered him, what if it got landed on a desk of corrupt officer. They would cover this up and again chances of Alex would become zero. Alex strained his head, as there had to someone who could help. Remember that friend of Alex, Edward from Angelano Chronicle was the man coming back to his head. He called.

Edward said, "Alex, it's good to know you are still safe. And your case is also calming down, as I get to hear from some of my Policemen friends and junior reporters. There was something I didn't told you the other day we spoke. Alex I have a friend who can smuggle you out of this country. Trust me, a new life at a new place is best bet."

Alex snapped back, "I am not leaving hot girls of Angelano behind. To be correct all girls of Angelano."

Edward concerningly said, "Alex, there are girls in every part of world, but not Angelano Police."

Alex said softly, "I think I have found the drug lord, and I also have evidences against him. Need your help. I want you to run a cover story on National TV, about exposing of Police of Commissioner who is running the drug syndicate. Yes that's him, and I have proofs with me."

Edward blew a breath, "Alex, I hope you aren't taking this accusation seriously and have started drugs."

Alex said, "Ah, haven't started drugs, but not been able to hit clubs though. Tell me how can you help."

Angelano chronicle was the best place to get this story featured, after all it was the top Media house of the city, and once something got aired on it, everybody followed. At first Edward didn't believe, but after seeing the evidences, he felt that story of his lifetime was this one, the similar feeling once Audrey had, but Edward was not going to die. In fact death penalty was waiting for the drug syndicate and Jody.

Edward said yes, and Alex felt like winning the war. At least his one accusation of being the drug lord would go off with this story, and who knew if Police or DEA or FBI would be able to make Jody confess on Audrey's death too. Everything was lining in place after all. In minutes Edward called his boss to tell him about this story. By the way, this boss was a top businessman of Angelano and also a competitive candidate to Mayor, and it took Edward a conversation of 5 minutes to convince him to run the story. Everything got in place, while Alex had turned on his TV to finally see something of his interest.

His eyes were all set, but wait what was that, a coverage on how snakes mated, a viral video of a cat slapping a dog, a story about world going to end in 5 years, a footage of one legged man dancing in a club. What the hell was that, seriously, Alex thought, he had given the best story ever to be broadcasted on National TV with so much of spice about Police Commissioner being the Drug Lord of

Angelano, and these idiots were showing how snakes mated! I mean it was interesting to see how animals did, as it could give some inspiration on new poses to try, but this was not the time, I mean it was night, and time to get in bed with clothes out, but Jody, show the freaking face of Jody covered with mikes but nothing to say. Alex thought, that Edward can't do this to him, Edward can't cheat, he was a professional first and friend later, so he would cover the story by its merit, and it had so much of merit. Wait Edward was a professional first, and friend later, no, no, he was both at the same time, but why wasn't exposing of Jody on air. Alex, kept the remote on his side while TV was buzzing with story on how a chameleon changes its color. Seriously, Alex thought, what a great timing.

'Breaking News', the voice came from TV to lit up Alex. The anchor on channel said, 'We just have got a tip from one of our reporters, indicating that our own Commissioner of Police might be city's most wanted drug lord. Can you believe it! This is surely dope at first sight, but you got to see this.'. The anchor then played recording, a teenager took our stuff earlier this day and has gone critical. Whoa, Jody you double faced prick, you have been poisoning the city, shame on you.

Alex jumped from his seat and started dancing, 'That's the way, ah haan, That's the way ah haan.'

He turned the channel, and again they were playing a story on Jody. 'This man might be known as the commissioner of Police, but he also has another identity. Drug Lord. Yes he runs a drug syndicate, and we are still running numbers on how many young lives we have lost because of this man. See this picture of him with a seasoned criminal Chih Ming Ho. Don't know him, worry not, just go to Chinatown and ask anybody where to get drugs from, and you will know who Chih Ming Ho is. Jody shame on you, and you are not getting away this time.

Edward called and said, "See this is how I help, and I take my words back. No need to go anywhere."

Alex said, "Man seriously, I have never wished kissing another man, but here you are. This is just the start, This Jody will regret messing up with me, and killing Audrey before that special night. I mean totally killing Audrey."

Edward said, "Hey I have calls coming, these people are asking for the evidences. Will get back later."

The city had gone upside down just within a night. A reporter on some local channel had even shot a picture of Jody screaming on phone in his balcony. Another reporter had seen Jody's lawyers coming to his house. Media had already reached the port office of First Freight. A new popup came on news channel, that FBI and DEA had both raided Jody's house. The mayor of Angelano who always pretended to be a Bestie of Jody was now giving statements like this, 'I am shocked to see the monster that lives inside Jody. May god help him, because I will make sure that every enemy of this city and law gets his due treatment. People like Jody are parasites, they will grow on you and one day will consume you, but not in Angelano. This is the city of peace, this is the city of Joy, this is the city of sunshine, we will not let Angelano be taken over by criminals.'

Seriously, what about who killed Audrey, was something this Mayor was missing. Some channels were already running story of Jody's life, his childhood pictures from Facebook, his career cases from Police Department, and his love life. Wait why was receptionist not on air, seriously if she could only tell her pain of being crushed, people would develop a serious hate against him. Oh shoot, there it was, on air, a FBI officer smelling oversized bras recovered from Jody's office. They suspected if drugs were being smuggled in these bras. This was the happiest moment of Alex's life, coming out winning from a dead end.

Alex called his dad. He said, "Alex, where are you. Did you saw the news. I can't believe The Angelano Police is itself the drug syndicate, and they were blaming on you. I thought only I was unjust to you."

Alex smiled, "Dad soon this all will be over. I will be up and running, and chasing uh my life."

Alex's dad said, "Why are you always so late? And also just get over with getting laid, this one is laid. Okay."

~~

Chapter 9

Alex couldn't sleep because of this over dose of joy. Yeah, it sounded well, the real Drug Lord was caught, and obviously Jody would tell them who killed Audrey, and who transferred money into Eddie's account, and who killed Terry, everything would come out easily. For the first time, hotel's coffee and eggs were smelling good. Ah, the first thing Alex thought of doing was, visiting Stella, she was an old friend of Alex, or precisely had slept with him couple of times and always loved doing it. Wait, Alex thought on why does it always had to end in bed, Audrey's body, and Stella's body, and everybody. Maybe he would just hit the beach, eat some ice cream with whipped cream. Ah, that looked nice.

But wait, Alex had to do something more important, surrender himself to Police and tell them his side of story. Yeah, that was more important, because officially he was still a wanted criminal, and it would be a shame if he died in a police encounter before sleeping with 100 women. Well, as it is said, this was the goal Alex had made in his life, 100 women to sleep with before he died. Sounded crazy, but for Alex, this was the real deal. Alex thought, how about some TV, and see helpless face of Jody in handcuffs. He turned the TV on.

Yeah, still the same story was on, about Jody. But wait what, Jody was screaming on National TV. 'I did nothing, these are false accusations. I can never in my dreams even sell cocaine. This is a cheap trick to defame me. I will fight my case with honor, and as I have already justified myself, there is nothing more to say.', while the anchor said, 'We are sorry Jody, but this scoop was irresistible. What do you say people, did you really believed if Jody was a drug Lord. Vote Yes or No, on our hotlines.'. What the F, was this voting about. Alex called Edward.

Edward said, "Alex, I could have lost my job, my career could have got doomed. But the good news is that Jody is no more the commissioner, so I feel safe a bit."

Alex was confused, "What do you mean, by he is not commissioner anymore and this scoop was fake."

Edward exhaled, "Alex, Commissioner did run the drugs business and that kid who got critical was also true. But he is running drug business of Chinese Medicine for sexual problems. I know it sounds crazy. Some of my sources say, he is doing a great cover up. But then he has proved his point. So it's the end."

Alex said, "What, Chinese medicine for sexual problems. Oh come on no one needs them, especially when Angelano chicks are just so hot, they can straighten anything."

Alex continued, "But what about that picture with Chih Ming Ho. That can't be lie."

Edward said, "I don't know. He is saying, that this picture was 5 years old when he was an undercover cop on a federal mission. That is how he got that picture, and Chih Ming Ho was a federal informer."

Alex said, "Come on who the hell will keep pictures of undercover mission in an album."

Edward said, "Same man who can keep oversized bras in his office locker. Guess so."

Alex said, "And what about First Freight. I saw found traces of drugs, or cocaine in their container."

Edward said, "Alex, this is what has saved majority of Journalists of Angelano from getting sued by Jody. First Freight and that Drug company is an illegal business, and that is why he is being pulled down by authorities. You can get a medal for this, if you want. But it changes nothing, you are still drug lord and Audrey's killer. Getting it."

The happiest days don't last long, maybe this was true, also that nothing is permanent, and change is the only truth. But change that fast, I mean faster than how people changed clothes after sex. This was unjust. God, Alex thought, after all this nothing changed. Why just me, God, this time seriously, why just me. Wait, but the money that came in Eddie's account was from First Freight. Someone was playing games, maybe this all was a cover up, and most probably that Jody knew who the criminal was, but would not say, until he was pushed. Maybe it was time that Alex gifted him oversized men undies, and tell him to get used to its smell, which was better than of prison cells. No way, Jody was getting away with murder of Audrey. He might have friends at high places that protected him now, but Alex was not going to back off.

But wait, what were the options. His career was now gone, so had nothing to fear of. His business was confiscated, so he would surely be mad at people. His oversized bras were found, so he, wait, that shouldn't concern him, but if it did, he would sure be looking for one size bigger, but at this time, no. If only at this time, Alex could hit at the right spot, Jody would vomit everything. But everything of Jody was gone, so what was it that Jody would now not want to lose. Maybe his pretty wife, oh no, if he loved her, he wouldn't be making museums of bras in his office. Then what was it, ancestral property, nah, as per Edward he had many assets in name of his family members throughout the country. Wait, there was something he cared about, After all the pictures in his office, and in his study should depict so. Yeah it was his daughter. No father would want to lose his daughter to Alex, not to Alex, but to anyone. So there it was, now target was Jody's daughter.

Alex started following his daughter, to school, to music classes, to swimming classes, to back home, to friends house, etc. etc. She was 7 year old, but was damn smart than her age. Now hiring a hit man wouldn't have worked in this case, because Alex was in no mood of killing the daughter and become a hardened criminal. He made his mind and did the preparations. The plan was set. He reached at Jody's daughter, Jade's school. The school got over and Jade was headed to her school bus when she saw Alex calling her by waving candies.

Jade said, "Hey, how much is that for. I want three candies, no, four, no wait for Arya too, five candies."

Alex felt insulted but controlled, "Hey sweetie, I am not selling them. But i got them for you, for free."

Jade wiped her nose, "But I don't take free things. We are rich people and we know everything comes for a price. So what's your price. Tell me, you poor candy seller."

Alex coughed a bit, "Okay, okay. You can pay me one cent. Or you can pay me when you get home, while I will ride you home in my car. See it's there."

Jade threw a cent at Alex, and snatched the candies. "I knew you and your candies were cheap."

Jade rushed back to her bus, while Alex felt like a deprived kid in front of a real kid. Seriously, What the F was this. Is this a girl, or some judgmental maniac? This is what Jody was teaching her beloved kid, to talk rudely, throw money at people, and boast of being rich. It was till this date, Alex thought he was the naughtiest kid he knew, but this girl was evil. Seriously, Alex thought what was wrong with kids these days. This girl turned out to be tougher than Jody himself. Man what will she be like when she grew up. While making out she would say, we are rich people, we don't like cocks, we eat turkeys, grrh. But wait, she was still a 7 year old girl, and they don't have much IQ.

What if one chance was gone, Alex knew everything about her, so he would try again, and after having fooled 20 something, 30 something, 40 something, and 50 no she wasn't 50, something women, what would a crazy rich kid would do to stop him. Alex got into his car, and followed Jade till her home. She then went out to music classes, which was near her house, dropped by her maid, who would return back right after 2 hours to pick her. Ah, Alex hoped, here she should be little more harmonious than school. Alex waited outside the school and then quietly skipped in. The classes had started, and Alex told the reception that he was a new parent looking to enroll his kid in these classes. He waived at Jade with guitar in his hand, who was talking to another kid of her class. Both approached him.

Jade said, "Hey you, poor singer, sing us a song, and I will pay you one more cent."

Alex said, "Hey sweetie, I am not poor. See this is a guitar, only rich people have it, like prince charming from Disney movie, and I don't need your cent. I want you to hear my music, but in my car."

Jade pointed at him, "You are not only poor but liar too. You got this guitar from one cent I gave you. Huh."

Alex surprisingly said, "Okay I will sing you a song, then you will sing back in my car. There are more instruments I have back in my car, you will love it."

Alex sang and before he could even complete a phrase, Jade threw another cent at him. Jade said, "You deserved this one cent for such a cheap singing. Buy another guitar and practice before coming next time."

The other kid said, "Hey lets go, teacher is playing our favorite."

Alex could only murmur, F You, and they went away running back to their teachers. Alex thought, seriously what is this kid, daughter of Satan, of course she had to be, as Jody could only be her worldly father. But Jody's wife seemed to be pretty to have such a nasty daughter, where did her DNA come from. Oh my god, Poor, Poor, Poor, Alex never felt that poorer. He actually felt that before all of this he was a janitor at High Rise who seriously stole Christie's soaps. Wait, the janitor at High Rise could be the person who stole Christie's soap. Many times he had told about fantasies for Christie. Whatever, but this kid was way beyond reach. Alex thought, seriously exposing her father was easier than getting this girl to his car. Alex thought, did he really played that bad the guitar. If so, his future relationship with Mia was already in troubled waters. Thanks God, Alex thought that he played Guitar for the first time not in front of Mia, or in any case in front of any girl, considering Jade was not a qualified to be a girl.

Chance at school was gone, now the chance of Music classes was also gone, damn it. What did this girl ate, probably money that too coins, or precisely a bowl full of one cents. But Alex was not giving up, as one more chance was there, to catch up with this girl at swimming classes. Yeah, Alex thought of giving this girl some time, and maybe on meeting third time she would not get judgmental about Alex's poorness. Wait, Alex thought, I wasn't poor, I have five properties to my name, and 400K plan, how could I be poor, and why do I even need to justify.

Alex waited for the servant to pick Jade, get back home, and again come out to drop Jade at swimming classes which again was near their house. She was supposed to pick back Jade after 1 and half hour. This time was just enough for Alex. Again Alex pretended to be father of a young boy who wanted to enroll his son into these classes, but the receptionist told him it was only girls, to which Alex said, he would then consider enrolling her niece. Of course making new kids or least pretending making new kids was something Alex was good at. Alex waved his hands to Jade, with a trophy in his hands. Jade approached him.

Jade said, "Poor people are losers, so you can't have a trophy, where did you steal it from."

Alex exhaled and said, "Hey sweetie, this is not mine. But this is for you, for being a good kid."

Jade snapped back, "If you have a trophy for me. I have something for you too."

Jade threw another one cent coin on Alex's face. This was outrageous, Alex held Jade's hands tightly and said, "Listen kiddo, this is not funny. I think you aren't aware what happened to your dad."

Jade jolted her hands out from his grip, "What happened to daddy, is he all right."

Alex took the chance and said, "Ah, no, no, no. He is all right, well not all – right, but little troubled. And kiddo, he needs you most now. So why don't we leave this freaking swimming classes and go see your daddy."

After all the encounters with Jade, Alex hadn't hoped for it, but it worked, Jade held Alex's hand and started walking. Everything was back in plan, but wait the swimming instructor came running towards them to see them leave. Alex panicked, if she had recognized his face. He left Jade's hand and started creeping towards the corner.

Instructor said, "Hey Mr. Who are you, and where are you taking Jade."

Alex stood dumbfounded while Jade spoke. "Oh Teacher, he is a poor friend, and we're going to see my daddy."

Alex felt both angry and little relieved, angry for again been called poor and relieved as this Satan had just saved him. Seriously, after everything Alex tried, what worked was, Daddy is unwell. This tough kid actually melted for her father. How unreal it was, if Alex was in her place he would have thrown another cent, wait, no Alex loved his father too, even more than Jade, and his father wasn't corrupt. The plan was working. Alex got Jade into his car, and they got moving around the streets of Angelano. Alex was driving around and killing time, for maid to reach swimming classes, find Jade missing, and then tell everyone that Jade was missing. It was then Alex would make a move, after Jody would get another panic attack. It was after a long that Alex was driving around Angelano. Yeah I mean, five six days were long enough for a man who would give lift to girls no matter where they were headed to the city. This habit of Alex had made him know every nook and corner of the city. Maybe it was this habit which was keeping him away from most patrolled streets by Angelano PD. Seriously everything was perfect, night, a proper win, well not that proper, but you had to act thug against a thug, and a long drive.

Alex looked back and felt relieved to see Jade calm and playing with toys, actually she was breaking them. Once a Satan, always a Satan. Alex thought on what would be Jody's first reaction, oh my little girl is gone, ha, ha, maybe then he would realize that women whose oversized bras he kept were also little girl of somebody. Well, okay, let's not get there, Alex thought. Maybe this pleasant night needed a song, so he turned on the radio. Whoa, it was

Whenever, Whatever by Mia. In seconds Alex got the vibes and started grooving. Meanwhile Jade tapped on Alex's shoulder to make him turn.

Jade said, "Why are you dancing, do you like this song?"

Alex said, "Hey sweetie, yes. You know she is the best singer in town, and soon we will be together. Just me, Mia, and lots of late night playlists. Well you tell isn't her voice melodious."

Jade said, "Yeah, it reminds me of my dad's karaoke sessions. I bet you must have heard them. Anyways take this."

Alex looked at his hands and five one cents. This time there was no stopping him, "Listen kiddo. I think you should save these cents for your daddy. It will buy him cigarettes in jail."

Jade snapped back, "I was giving these cents to you, because I thought we would run out of gas, and as you are poor, you might not have money for more gas. We are done now. Take me back home."

Alex frowned and thought, seriously was this supposed to be a nice gesture. What is this girl, does she owns a bank that only has one cents. Seriously, she was the first girl that Alex had met who thought she was rich, but only had heaps of one cents. And 5 cents, who the hell will give me gas of 5 cents, for a car. Alex thought, maybe I was wrong, this girl isn't Satan, she is retarded. All 7 year old girls know how much gas costs, and this freaking Barbie is telling me to refill the tank with 5 cents. Phew, where am I stuck, Alex thought. For a minute it crossed his mind, if Jody would be even interested in confessing against the security of his retarded girl. God please, make me believe that she is only acting weird in front of me, and she doesn't pays her parents one cent every time they kissed her.

Meanwhile Jade yelled from back, Take me back home. Whoa, whoa, this was not good, Alex thought, because if she kept yelling, people would soon make this car stop and the plan will be blown. Wait, why was Alex scared of this retarded Satan, he instead of making her quiet, increased the volume of radio. Now it was perfect. Ah, Alex prayed a little prayer to God, to never ever give him a daughter like this, or he would, what would I do, yes, or I would throw cents on face of Holy mother of Jesus, Mary, every time he would visit the church, Yeah, on the face.

Alex looked at his watch, it has been 2 and half hours since he drive off the swimming classes. Yeah, the time was right. By now Jody must have been started to freak out. Alex looked back and saw Jade again playing with toys. He turned the volume down and dialed Jody's number. The time has came for that prick to go to jail.

Alex said, "Listen you prick, enough of your games with me. Now I hope you are enjoying mine. I have got you out of Commissioner's office. I have got your First Freight drown. I have fantasized your pretty wife, wait I haven't, only with a morphed body. You listen, I have your girl, and you will do exactly as I say."

Jody yelled, "Hey, you have no idea whom you are messing with. She is my girl, getting it."

Of Course, Alex thought and said, "Listen, now do as I say. Walk out, get in your car, drive to District Attorney's office, and confess that you killed Audrey, Terry, and you are the drug lord."

A voice came from back, "I think he is Audrey's brother. He came looking for you."

Jody said, "Oh boy, please don't take it personally. Audrey would be mad seeing you do this."

~

Chapter 10

For a while they fought, they negotiated, they avoided, they calmly talked, they yelled, they got confused. But Alex was clear, that was not getting down to any terms laid by Jody. This commissioner's time was done now. Well Jody was for sure sounding scared, as if his time has come up. Jade was just listening, and probably was in shock to hear Alex yelling at her parents. She didn't moved an inch, then suddenly started beating Alex's back.

Alex yelled at phone, "I will give you one cent. Uh, I mean one chance. You either do this, or I will cut your daughter into pieces smaller than 1 cent, and throw them in your garden for your own dogs to eat it."

A voice came from behind Jody, "But we don't have dogs."

Jody calmly said, "Okay, I am going out to drive to District Attorney and confess as you say."

Alex hung up the phone. Yes, Whoa, Yes, the feeling was unparalleled. He looked back at Jade and frowned at her face without even a bit of pity that Alex was just sending her Dad to Jail. Seriously, pity for what, a cold blooded murderer, who killed Audrey on a love making night. I mean who kills that sexy a girl on a bed, when you have thousand other things to do. Wait, while Alex had thousand other things to do, but her father didn't let that happen. What starts as evil, ends with evil, this was the new age karma which had to applied on Jody.

Alex started driving towards a warehouse he had rented, to hide the girl, the retarded Satan. Alex thought, tomorrow will be a new morning, when the culprit will be jailed, and Alex will be free as ever hitting on even hotter girls. Seriously, it all looked like a dream, where Alex was the hero who had successfully brought down an evil empire. Maybe Angelano Film industry should make a film on his this part of life, on how Alex proved his innocence. Alex never in his dreams had thought that he could be fiercer than a police commissioner, wilder than a murderer, and crazier than a drug lord, well all three were the same though. Ah, maybe he would also get some reward, or some sorts of medal from Angelano Govt. as Edward said, for exposing such grave crimes and criminal, and they would be definitely pricier than 1 cent, Ha! Alex took out his phone, the other one, and switched it on to call Edward. He noticed it had 13 missed calls. Whoa, somebody was missing him badly. He called him back.

Marvin said, "Alex, Alex, where have you been man. I have something you might want to know badly."

Alex smiled, "Oh, its nice to talk to a friend, after all, the crap in my life is flushed out. You know what, I have just made that Police Commissioner confess to his crimes. Ha, just a night more, and I will take you to the hottest club of town tomorrow. Just get your best outfit together."

Marvin interrupted, "Alex that's what I wanted to tell you. Its not Commissioner, the Jody, no."

Alex braked the car and said, "Hey, hey, hey, what are you saying. Its not Jody, but he admits to his crimes."

Marvin said, "I don't know that. But the account number which I hacked for details from Bank of Bahamas was wrong. The account I got details from was MH9332456LP. The nine in it was actually 8, so the right account number was MH8332456LP. The account holders name that transferred that shit money is Rubin Maestro."

Alex bumped his hands on steering making a horn noise that scared him for a second. He said, "F you Marvin, you are telling me this now. F you, I have kidnapped his daughter, and all that news on TV about Jody, I was behind it. You have any idea, how badly you have screwed this up. God."

Marvin said, "Not much though, you are just a kidnapping more to your crime records."

Alex hung up the phone, and rested his temple on the steering. Shit, shit, everything is back as before. Alex thought, I am still a wanted criminal. Wait, but what if Jody confessed his crimes. He would be able to walk away free. No, Alex thought that this was wrong, especially he couldn't just afford another crime charge of kidnapping. He drove back to Jody's neighborhood, but there was already lot of Police. It was not hard to guess that Jody hadn't gone to District attorney, but had called the Police. But it didn't mattered anymore, I mean why would it, another kidnapping would be no big deal for a city wide drug lord. Shit, yes it was. Alex was not a criminal, and everything he did to prove it wrong, turned up against him. Alex looked back at the Jade, and god if anything happened to this girl now, Alex was gone forever. He drove towards the swimming classes, and found a spot far from public eyes. He dropped Jade, looked around, and drove back towards his hotel.

Alex thought, shit another crime it was to his name. He looked up, beyond the car's roof, to god, and thought when I wanted to be a playboy you never gave me girls, but now when I don't want to be blamed as a criminal you are giving me every crime that is possible. Why god, why. Damn it. Alex thought what damage he had done to Jody. Probably Jody was just another Tax saving guy who didn't wanted to pay taxes for First Freight, and Alex just not only kaput his company, but also took his elite Police Job.

Finally Alex did something wrong he didn't believed in. Will ever Alex be able to get out of this mess, and maybe go back on a day job again, well it didn't looked like that. Alex's phone rang, and he picked.

Edward said, "Alex, are you out of your mind. You kidnapped Jody's daughter. What were you thinking?"

Alex said, "Oh I wanted to adopt her, but Jody wouldn't let that happen, so i took her. Fair enough. What the F do you think I kidnapped his daughter, Of course to make him confess for his crimes which apparently he didn't do. I screwed up bad time, Edward I am a dead man."

Edward breathed, "Relax, Its not over yet. I know a detective in Angelano PD, why don't I fix up a meeting of yours with him, and you can tell your side of story to him."

Alex said, "And what will I tell, that I hacked the bank of Bahamas but hey no war got started."

Edward said, "Phew. Alex what do you want to do, apart from shadowing the National TV with your crimes."

Alex said, "I just know one thing that Audrey died, Terry Died, and I didn't do it, but they died, so there has to somebody who is doing this, and I need to find him. Hey listen I got to go, but I'll call you."

Alex was back in his hotel room, and it was never that dark. Everything looked falling apart. Alex took out his mobile phone and did a Google search 'Who is the Drug Lord of Angelano', and voila the search results started coming in, It is Alex, an ex-marketer, it is Alex who is also assumed to have killed a young girl Audrey, and even the Google was saying that it was him. Hell, this Google always helped, but now it too was against Alex. Seriously, only because Alex didn't had control on his pants, he hit the club, and took Audrey to the hotel room. It was all because of his nasty pants that he was in such situation. Alex furiously punched in between his pants, and started moaning when he felt it.

God, am I becoming mad. Alex thought, of everything he did, he was again back to ground zero. Bringing down commissioner, inquiring the hit man, kidnapping Jody's daughter, all went in vain. Alex thought, only if Audrey would have been alive she could have told who killed her, wait if she was alive how would she be killed, wait, wait, Audrey, yes Audrey could have known who killed her. She was investigative journalist after all, and if she was even closely as good as Alex in her job, she would have known who might hurt her. Yes, Alex stood up on his bed. But how to know what Audrey knew. There was one way of doing that. If Alex got hands on her research work for this story, he could get hints on who killed her, or who the drug lord was, and that research work would possibly still be there in her house on her study. Alex, made up his mind to get hands on her research work for story.

Alex called Edward and said, "You are a Journalist, and I am sure you must know all journalists around the city."

Edward said, "Well not all, but I can connect you with anyone."

Alex snapped back, "I need Audrey's address, and not the graveyard where she might be resting, but the place where she lived before this all happened."

Edward knew a friend from Audrey's organization and got the address for Alex. It was an apartment in downtown, first floor. But there was a problem that Audrey didn't lived alone, she also had a room mate and the room mate still lived there. But wait, if Alex could handle Jade, what would this roommate could possibly do. Ha, Alex got on his car, and in few odd minutes he was waiting down the apartment building. The lights were on, and possibly there was some man inside the flat. Alex thought, maybe he should have listened to Audrey, when she was saying that lets go to my apartment, but then Alex wanted to act professional by taking her to hotel room.

Damn, why didn't he got her to her own apartment, least he would be hitting the clubs now. Alex waited, and also listened to music been played in the apartment. Soon the lights went off and Alex saw a tall man exiting the building. Alex waited for another hour, for the room mate to go to sleep, so he could enter quietly. It was now he could even listen the leaves whistling. Alex got out of the car, and started climbing the balcony of apartment. He noticed that some light was coming from the living room, but it was all quiet, so he assumed it must lamps. He quietly slid a knife in hinge of door and opened it. He slid it aside and saw somebody in dark was watching porn on TV, and note that it was silent Porn, or wait the volume was turned off. Alex panicked and stumbled, while the lights went on and a girl was sliding up her Pajamas.

The girl shouted, "Hey, who are you. Did you come here to steal something?"

Alex got scared as she might wake other neighbors, so he closed the door and approached her, while she threw a vase on his head. Alex screamed silently, and got hold of her. Alex said, "Hey listen, I am not a thief, in fact I have a bigger apartment than you, and much bigger collection of porn I used to have in college. I am just here to talk."

The girl then realized that it was Alex, and said, "Hey you are the one, you killed Audrey."

Girl punched hard in Alex's belly, while Alex gripped her arms tightly. Alex said, "Yes I am Alex, and I didn't killed Audrey. For god sake, she went up to that room to sleep with me."

Girl was still in his grip and yelled, "Oh so you think she was a slut."

Alex held her back pushing to his chest, "No, because if every girl that I sleep with is a slut, then this city's every girl would be slut, and Angelano would called, Slutenano. Ah, that's bad, I might be exaggerating, but the point is that I didn't killed Audrey. In fact I want to find her killer, and I need your help."

Girl started panting, "How could I help you, apart from making this city be called Slutenano. You freak."

Girl nudged him hard and Alex got hold of it. Alex said, "Okay, okay, time out. Listen, I just need the research work of story Audrey was working on, and I will be gone. And do you really think, with Police after me, I would visit one of my victim's house to collect some paper work. Think girl, think."

Girl calmed and said, "Okay, time out. I can give that to you."

Both got separated from tussle, and stood apart facing each other for few minutes catching up with breaths. The girl walked inside another room, while Alex looked around. Ah, there it was pictures of Audrey hung on wall. She was looking as pretty as the other day, wait there was also one in bikini, and damn she looked hot in it. Wait, Alex tried remembering on how did she looked that night without her clothes, but couldn't remember a thing. He thought, did he even did anything with Audrey. Seriously what could be worse than trying to nail somebody, and land up in your own coffin.

Alex saw a card framed with Audrey and this wild wild girl. Probably her name was Ashley. Seriously, if Alex had missed one of her moves, he would never be able to take stands on nights. This was close. Seriously, did all girls of Angelano knew face of Alex. God, there was too much of damage control to be done. Alex peeped into one of the bedroom that had door open, and saw the bed which looked comfier than that hotel one. What a shame, as he didn't listened to Audrey that night. Alex waited for another minute then curiously went towards Ashley, who just appeared back. She had got a box full of CD's, files, pictures, and folders. That was it, her research behind her last big story. Ashley looked at Alex and slowly drew something out from box. It was a bottle of wine.

Ashley said, "Maybe some wine, Mr. Innocent. Or maybe your last wine, if proven guilty."

Alex said, "Ah, you know what. There is no power in this world that can keep me away from girls. Well but an exception would be if they keep me in coed prison. Ha, but that doesn't happens, exactly like an innocent man never gets convicted in Angelano. I have my faith in this city of angels, yeah, still I do."

Ashley said, "Oh it's nice to know about your faith. By the way, apart from girls, what else interests you."

Alex thought for a while and said, "I guess more girls, and of course having wine with them."

Ashley couldn't help but smile, "So this is how you get women to hotel rooms."

Alex said, "Well that is a serious accusation, apart from being a drug Lord. You know what, sometimes, women take me to hotel rooms, sometimes to their homes, and sometimes even i become the victim. I am sure you must be watching the news lately. By the way, I am not sure, who got this bottle of wine here."

Ashley grinned, and they talked. Ashley told him that she was a Jewelry designer, and how badly she loved her job. Most of the times she worked from home, and so this apartment was like a temple for her. While Ashley told him, Alex couldn't help but look at the Porn DVD kept on the couch. Seriously, this had to be a modern age temple, or more of an Indian Kama temple. They even talked a little about Audrey, who always wanted to break stories, right from geyser not working to global warming beyond limits. As per Ashley, Audrey never trusted men that easily. In fact she had broken up with her ex just because of trust issue. Ashley also told him, that it was her who told the police that it was unlikely that Audrey would trust a man to be taken to a hotel room.

Alex thought, seriously, was he that special to have won the trust of Audrey. I mean what could be the reason that Audrey went that easily to the hotel room, when she had trust issues. Maybe, that night was supposed to be that way, or Alex's skill of wooing women was just getting better and better. For proofs, it was getting obvious that something for sure was going to happen tonight between Alex and Ashley, but Alex not a moment let that to appear. They were already one bottle down, and Ashley got the second bottle of wine. Seriously, this had to be the best night since Alex was on run. Ah, he hadn't even hit the club and had a woman by his side.

Ashley said, "I don't understand one thing. You both were in the same hotel room. Then Audrey gets killed, and you go on a run. Still you claim that you are innocent. What do you have apart from charming talks to prove it."

Alex said, "Seriously. I had a clean criminal record all my life. Murder weapon isn't found. I was doing a staged drug deal when Terry was killed, but still police thinks I could have been at two places at same time. Money transferred to the hit man who tried taking out the detective was not from my account. And there is heap of arguments to that."

Ashley said, "So keep it simple, surrender yourself to police and see them in court."

Alex said, "Ah I wish I hadn't run, now it's too late. You know Audrey said, Police is corrupt, and I just panicked."

Ashley said, "What if I say that you stop running. I hope you wouldn't panic tonight."

That was it, Ashley lips had come just too close to Alex's, and they kissed. In fact this kiss appeared to Alex like a crime for many reasons. First it was inappropriate, as Alex was here for evidences not sex. Second, Ashley was friend of Audrey, but wait Audrey wasn't around anymore, so it was okay. Third, Ashley was really wild and she was murdering Alex's pretty lips. Alex thought, maybe he got lucky tonight, but wait evidences were more important, but they could always wait for a night. Alex thought that being on run also had its perks, and he too kissed her hard. Slowly they unworn their clothes, and Ashley took him to the bedroom. Alex still couldn't believe that it was happening. But it was, and damn Ashley was way wilder than Audrey. Wished he had listened to Audrey and came to her apartment and met Ashley before and not like this. But anyways, meeting her like this also didn't matter.

Ashley said, "Ah, this is good. I just hope that tomorrow morning I don't rise up dead."

Alex said, "Seriously are you planning to sleep this night, because I am not".

~~

Chapter 11

Hope this was not a crime, Alex thought, because everything Alex had done after that night had happened to be a crime. But this was something beautiful. Especially the way Ashley stood in front of him, while Alex was feeling little dizzy while been spread on the bed. Ashley was slowly taking off her last of clothes, and that little pieces of earrings hat she had probably designed herself. Seriously this jewelry designer was a gem. Alex couldn't stop but smile at her. This night was a proof that being accused of crimes doesn't kill your chances with women. Maybe Ashley had a soft corner for Alex who had too much of troubles in his life now. Whatever it be, this night had started to get awesome. Ashley was making sexiest of moves, while slowly spreading her hands over her body. This was turning out to be best night of Alex. God might do bad things to you, but he also keeps surprises, and this one was just good.

Alex said, "Hey come on, you are taking too much of time. I can undress you in a blink of an eye."

Ashley said, "Nah, I am just making this night special for you. Who knows I might be the last girl you hit on."

Alex said, "Last girl to hit, hey we are not marrying right. I am not one of those, but Alex."

Ashley laughed loudly and picker her phone. She said, "As I said, you don't need to run anymore. Let me make it easy for you. He has picked the call. Hey detective Joe, how are you doing. I have somebody with me, whom you are looking for. Yeah, you got it, Alex. He is lying naked in my bedroom ready to be fucked by law. Yeah.

Please come over. He is all yours. Nah, he won't run, as I have told him not to. Yeah he trusts women. Ha ha."

The party was over for Alex, and he got drained of all joy. Alex screamed, while Ashley was still making little moves with her half naked body. By the way Ashley had just handcuffed Alex with sex toys to the bed. So he couldn't really run, and was just struggling to get off the bed.

Alex yelled, "Are you crazy. You called the Police. I should've known. Hey put off these handcuffs."

Ashley said, "Calm down Alex, we are not sleeping tonight, like you said. Ha ha."

Alex yelled with all the power he got, and started jumping on the bed. He too had got the wild vibes of Ashley, and with a good scream he stretched his hands with all his will, to break the handcuffs. He panted for a second, and stared at Ashley. He took his clothes, and ran towards the living room, while Ashley picked up the handcuffs and murmured, 'Cheap Online Toys'. Alex took the box containing research work of Audrey and rushed out from the door. He soon got in his car and was driving away. Alex thought, God that was close, what a freaking woman was she, too much influenced by storyline porn. Alex couldn't stop panting, and thinking how could he have trusted Ashley. Seriously, not every good looking woman is good, and how many times Alex had to accept this fact.

Wait, what if this Ashley blamed charges of Alex forcibly having sex with her. Damn, it would be another disaster. Ah, everything was screwing up badly for Alex. He thought, Ashley why did you do this. But wait, those few kisses, well those few good kisses, no, those few damn good kisses, though felt nice, and so did striptease of Ashley, but it wasn't worth his innocence. Already Joe Winslow was after his life, now he would get another reason to sham him. Alex reached his hotel, and scarily turned on the TV. Oh no, not again.

The anchor of News show was saying, "Fugitive Alex has done it again. He broke into the house of Audrey, and got physical by all means with her roommate Ashley. This monster, now needs to be stopped."

While Ashley who pretended to be a pretty girl was saying, "He is savage. He made me took off my clothes. He made me drink two bottles of wine, so he could sleep with me. He took all works of Audrey so Police couldn't find clues against him. He made me do all dirty things, by scaring me that he would do the same as he did to Audrey. I want this man behind bars, and be hung till death. This is what he deserves, not striptease. Uh, he also made me do that."

Alex covered his face with his hands, and felt all the shame of deeds he didn't do. Why God, why. Every time Alex thought of doing some good to prove himself innocent, it all turn against him. May be Edward was right, Alex was no detective, or Police, he was a marketer, and these things were better left to a professional. Maybe it was time that Alex stopped all this crusade of finding the killer, and surrendered himself to Police and let them do their job. But after all this mess, it had become more difficult to even put up a defense case in court. All these liars would line up and defame Alex, was what he feared.

But Alex wasn't scared of them. He thought maybe tomorrow morning he would call Edward and agree to speak with that detective. Was that right, of course it was right to do anything to save your back. Alex laid on bed, and remembered Marvin's call. Wait, who was this Rubin

Maestro. Before that Alex thought of juggling the box he had got from Audrey's apartment.

He saw a newspaper cutting, 'A rookie gets killed by a car bumping into him, owned by Rubin. A co-incidence or was Rubin's car as high as people in his parties?'.

There were few photographs of a tall man with face circled around, posing in front of few properties. With a paper was attached the ownership of that property, transferred from Mark Hunting to Rubin Maestro. Then there was another newspaper cutting that said, 'Popular hotelier Mark Hunting leaves Angelano forever'.

There was article that read, 'If Zeus is god of Sky, then Rubin is God of Angelano's nightlife'.

Another newspaper article read, 'Floor on Fire gets raided in suspect of being city's new hot spot for easy drugs. Rubin the owner denies all allegations. He says, if boys and girls can walk in, they can also walk in with drugs, and in hospitality it is considered rude to body check our guests. Maybe Police should start looking in our alleys.'.

This was not getting over as Alex saw more of them. Another article read, Attorney Steven Somber and his family dies in a house fire. He was the same man who was fighting legal case of extortion against Rubin Maestro.

Rubin, Rubin, and Rubin Maestro, this name was everywhere inside the box. In fact it was the only name in the box. Clearly Rubin couldn't have been boyfriend of Audrey to have her obsessed about him, so who was he, the drug Lord. It has to be. All this time Alex looked everywhere, but Rubin was right there, the number one suspect even in eyes of Audrey. Audrey was clearly after Rubin's back, so this man who got killed many others, could have easily got Audrey out of his way. Seriously, this man was pretty famous, but why didn't anybody told him about Rubin, who had such a huge crime record.

Something was wrong. In fact the Police too didn't suspected Rubin, the man who always got away with his crimes. Alex also found few pictures of Rubin with bunch of Policemen. No he wasn't arrested in that picture, but was having drinks with them. So the police was corrupted, and maybe that's why, was ignoring Rubin's involvement in this. Seriously he was the elephant in the room, or that oversized bra, that would catch any normal eye. Alex did a small Google search on Rubin Maestro, and there it was heaps of crime in his name, but no arrests, or no conviction. Wait, Rubin also had filed a case on Daily Mirror, the same newspaper where Audrey worked in. Makes sense, they were old rivals. No, no, no, the meeting with detective tomorrow can wait, but Alex knew he had to follow Rubin's tail, or again he would walk away.

Alex called Layla and said, "Layla, why didn't you tell me about Rubin Maestro, yes your boss. Instead you gave me lead of that poor Terry. I might not be the man of your dreams, but then I wasn't asking you to sleep with me."

Layla said, "Alex whatever I told you, I shouldn't have. You know I can get in trouble for this."

Alex said, "Trouble, seriously. What is worse, losing a job, or finding a prison? Of our small friendship, you didn't even think once, that you might be misleading me."

Layla exhaled, "Okay Yes, Rubin has a drug network, but nobody till this date has been able to prove it. Listen Alex, he is not a nice man. I don't know if he killed Audrey, but I am sure, if you bother him like Jody, he is gonna kill you. Again I am saying, its better you stay away from him."

Alex said, "You know what Layla, I have hit his club, I have hit girls in his club, and now I will hit him. You don't worry, just tell me whatever you know."

Layla said, "Okay, if you want to expose him. Your best bet would be through Alina or Larry."

These two weren't just names, but the building blocks of Rubin's empire. Larry was his accountant, but apart from running numbers, handling finance, he operated all on ground activities of Rubin. In fact hiring of local musicians like Mia, was also a part of Larry's job. That for sure made him lucky in eyes of Alex. If there was shortage of drug supply in any of clubs, Larry was the man to take care of. Goons that Rubin had under his control, got all their orders from Larry. All the properties that Rubin had seized illegally, was part of Larry's job, right from threatening the rightful owners, to creating ruckus for rightful owners, to manage the local police, to handle the law and order, to everything till Rubin procured it. Right from extortions to business settlements, Rubin did them all, and Larry was his operations guy. In fact First Freight's distribution channel was also handled by Rubin and Larry. Alex hadn't met him, but Larry's image was quite of a bold go getter guy, till he opened the website of Rubin's business that had a photo of lean, thin, and polite man. Yeah that was Larry on ground. Seriously, he did looked like an accountant, but more of a nerd without pimples. But Alex hadn't to sleep with him, so it didn't matter if Larry shaved his legs or not.

Next to Larry's picture, was a portrait of some sex goddess, seriously, was Alina that sexy as she looked in the portrait. Well now Alina was more of a business partner to Rubin. She was the people's women in all of Rubin's hotels, bars, restaurants, and primarily offices. She knew each of person employed by Rubin. Plus she also handled marketing for Rubin, ah Alex got touched and his belief that marketers were sexy as hell got firmer. Alina was the sole point of contact when it came to international clients, like meeting with them, greeting with them, sleeping with them, wait, not sleeping, as Layla wasn't sure about that. Alina was also the PR face of Rubin and maintained good repo with all leading politicians and govt. officials on Rubin's behalf. So this was his empire and people behind it.

Alex said, "So you think Larry could be the person behind all of my miseries, and I need to reconsider my target."

Layla said, "No. Larry is like a computer program, and everything Rubin feeds, he runs like that. Trust me, Rubin is like a Lion, with no weaknesses, no vulnerabilities, and bunch of bodyguards always surrounding him. But if you can break through these two people, you can hunt this Lion."

Alex said, "Okay. So I am a hunter, he is a lion, and no way we are sleeping together. I mean, I and Lion, I and Rubin, not us two. Because I still believe we could be a great pair. Thanks Layla, will stay in touch."

Alex had 2 options, of either collecting strongest of evidences against Rubin, or make him confess. He thought, he would try both, and see which one of works. After a day of catching up with tails of Rubin, Alina, and Larry, Alex got to know that Layla was damn right. This Rubin was like a ghost. Inspite of being one of the richest man in Angelano, catching his sight was like seeing a comet, as even if you did saw him, he would be gone before you recognize. But Larry and Alina were all over the town.

Alex's first target was Larry, and he started following him like a shadow. Everywhere he went, Alex would be few cars behind, or few pillars behind, or few people behind. Everything appeared bleak to this Mafia Empire of Rubin. Alex knew he was messing with the bad boy, and consequences could be graver than messing up with a girl's ex-boyfriend. But did he have a choice, No. Today Larry was meeting with all of Rubin's drug peddlers. Alex had photographed all his meetings, and exchanges of brown packets, of which one peddler gave Alex the glimpse of cocaine by pulling the real thing out. It was all captured. Seriously these people were as casual like if they were exchanging some hot girl's numbers, and guess what in one of the exchanges there was also a policeman accompanying them who too got pictured in Alex's camera. Alex noticed a peddler who was mid aged, and had a 10 year or so kid with him. Once Larry exited Alex went in, and gave a candy to the kid.

Alex said, "Hey this is for you champ. Trust me, the only thing it kills is sourness of mouth."

The peddler snapped back with the baseball bat in his hand, "And do you know what this kills is anybody who messes with my kid, especially strangers. Back off."

Alex stood up and said, "Nice, a bat for your kid, and a back to all those dying but others kids. Hmm".

Peddler calmed and took his kid behind him, "Hey listen, I don't show my back to dying kids. I see them in their eyes, the same eyes that differentiate me and my kid from this society, and you know what I sell them death on their face. Huh, and they buy it with same smile, as you should give and walk away."

Alex said, "I will pay you money, grands of it. If you become my witness against Rubin."

Peddler started laughing, "Okay and what will I do with those grands, probably buy an ebony furnished coffin for my son. That would be perfect, least he will get a good after life."

Alex said, "Listen, I will protect you and your son too. But I just need your testimony."

Peddler chuckled, "You are not getting it right. Probably I am the first peddler you have seen with a kid, who could come at price for good life of his son. But there is no son, if you go against Rubin. Try ones that even don't have kids, they will too say a no, because they have balls, yes they have balls they don't want to lose. Stop wasting your time. Now I remember you, you are the same man accused of killing that girl in hotel. You will get nothing."

The peddler walked away, while Alex damned his luck. Seriously was this Rubin that hard a nut to crack. Ah, no one got balls of steel other than Super Man, and Rubin was not Super Man for sure. Like he did with girls, Alex thought of keep trying. He kept following Larry, tonight he was meeting with goons that did dirty work for Rubin. It must have been payout time. Alex thought, seriously he was outnumbered, but then he remembered the fact that he was always outnumbered, as to even when it came to luck with girls. This stuff was way more organized than Alex had ever thought. It appeared that everybody knew that they were going to get laid, and it made it simpler for them. Each man knew their job and was been paid for that. Rubin was a tough guy to crack. But Alex kept following.

Late at night, Larry stopped at a retail mart. He went inside, and loud noises started coming out. Few minutes later he came out verbally fighting with a man. This was getting serious. Few of the men with him had also loaded their guns. But Alex kept his calm. Then they talked for a while and Larry gave them a briefcase. What it could be, cocaine, or money, or maybe guns. Then Larry walked away. One thing was sure that Larry was no friend with these people, and obviously as Layla had said that Larry was computer program, so these people would probably be no friends to Rubin as well. Alex waited for Larry to drive off and then approached the retail mart.

Alex said, "Ha. Every dog has his day, and every bitch has its night. Well, I mean every dog, you know who the dog is, and well there aren't bitches in here although its night. Strange isn't it. I am Alex. I saw you were fighting with that prick, and I just wanted to join you."

One man said, "You are late. He is gone. Tonight the bitch won't have her night." They started laughing loudly.

Alex said, "You know if there weren't any bitches, there would be no difference between days and nights."

The head of that group said, "I didn't knew that bitches too take LGBT rights seriously." They started laughing.

Alex exhaled, "I know this is your retail mart, and Rubin is taking over it illegally. I also know that dog fights won't help against him. So why don't bitches take their rights seriously, and nail that son of a gun, Rubin. I want you to become my witness, and testify against Rubin's crimes. I will pay in grands."

They started laughing while the head of them said, "Boy you bring down Rubin, and I will pay you double."

Alex smiled and said, "I don't know the code around here. But is that a deal?"

The head gravely said, "Yeah, unless you want to walk in and sleep over."

They again started laughing. But wait, this time Alex too shared a loud laugh with them. In fact he did walked in with them, though not to sleep, but to add their property legal papers along with pictures of them fighting as a proof of extortion racket of Rubin. Alex thought, ah thanks god these men didn't had a son to loose. He thought, Rubin, you are so gone, so gone, that we won't miss you ever.

~~

Chapter 12

This was going good, especially last night was a jackpot. Alex not only had convinced the retail mart owners to testify against Rubin, but the retail mart owners had also given Alex a copy of Mart's ownership. Seriously this was getting introduced to another hot girl by your girlfriend, because it rarely happened. But one thing was sure, that Alex wasn't the only one trying to bring down Rubin. After all these crime movies depicted the truth. The more dirtier you are, more enemies you got to have, and right now the best bet for Alex was to find such enemies. But seriously Alex pitied on that poor peddler father, who could only see ebony coffin and not gallows for Rubin.

But this wasn't over, Rubin had a very bad reputation of always walking free, and Alex had to ensure that he had enough proofs to get him locked. It was another day and Alex was again following Larry. Today Larry met with couple of Policemen, and they talked for a while, and in the end Larry gave them a huge hug with sliding something in their pocket. Though Alex captured them in his camera, but nothing was obvious apart from the fact that few Policemen were friends of an alleged criminal. Well that was enough. Alex followed him and Larry stopped at an old warehouse kind of building, while few women who looked like hookers passed by shaking hands with Larry.

Alex thought seriously, Hookers, this was the new low of Rubin's crimes. Alex hated prostitution, not because women were made to have sex just to fulfill their basic needs, yeah the other kind of basic needs. But he hated it because it undermined all the great efforts that men should put up in pursuit of sleeping with a woman. A appearing hooker stopped by Alex's car.

The hooker said, "Hey nice ride you got. By the way how much horse power it got."

Alex avoided and said, "Ah, enough to take me away to the right place. By the way I don't buy sex."

The hooker started yelling, "You shithole, what did you say. Do I look like a hooker? Guess what, today your mommy did my make-up. Hey you, get out of that car. And what did you say, you don't buy sex. Guess what, after today you are going to buy that thing you use to do sex. Get out of the car. I will tell you."

The windows were up, but this whore was causing too much of distraction. Even Larry had his neck turned around. So Alex just drove out, while the hooker kept yelling. Seriously, Alex just drove out, the same man who would never succumb to women, unless it's necessary to adjust with length of her legs. Alex thought, Ha, I will have to buy that thing, probably the same amount could have kept this hooker tied up to his bed. Seriously, why did even god made hookers, wait, not because God didn't had hitting skills, but maybe he might have got some other reasons. Alex had parked his car just around the block and waited for Larry to pass. He followed Larry again, and wait he was entering the port that meant Alex had to face again that security person. The security did stopped him.

The security said, "Sir, you were so right. First Freight is so closed."

Alex coughed, "Yeah I know, I know. See this is what happens when right things don't happen at right time, exactly like I am following my boss in that car ahead of me. I mean we are together, but if I don't make it there while he steps down on that port ground. You know what could happen."

The security guard said, "Another of Port company will shut down, right."

Alex whiffed, "Nah, I will lose my Job. Do you want that to happen."

The guard saluted and opened the check gate with all due respect, while Alex felt like yeah easier than hitting women. He followed Larry to a Ship which was about to leave the port. Something big was happening, Alex could sense it. Not because of the huge size of ship, but there were many shady men that greeted Larry. Alex looked closely, but couldn't see any arms with those men. Well that was good, but Larry appeared to be in hurry. He shook hands with a suited man who handed Larry few papers, which Larry gave to those shady men. Something was happening, and Alex had to find out.

Alex waited for Larry to get in his car and be moving. Alex slowly sneaked out and entered the ship with body language of a goon, and sturdiness of a porn star, wait not porn star but a murderer. Yes he did looked tough. But inside, whoa, were a line of most luxurious cars Alex had even seen at such distance. There were Ferraris, Bugati, Rolls Royce, and some freaking costly cars. Wait, but did Rubin also started a motor dealership. No he was too grey for a store visited by family men ready to pour their lives savings. Then the same shady man started keeping one of those papers inside the car. It clicked to Alex, that these were stolen cars with new forged papers. This Rubin's hands were dirtier than teens trying first time, wait, not all teens, except Alex who always had a classic master stroke. Alex noticed some boxes kept on other side of cars. He picked one of them and went ahead to keep in one of the cars. The shady man stopped him.

The shady man said, "Hey what are you doing? What is this box, some cookies for grandma?"

Alex said, "Ah. I don't know, maybe Larry wants the new owners to have a taste of his Grandma. Yeah, these boxes came from Larry's home. And he said, you can forget keeping those papers in cars, you can also forget keeping cars in this ship, but do not miss keeping these boxes. This is what I was told."

The shady man laughed, "Okay. Keep them. You look to be new, haven't seen you around."

Alex opened the door of a car and said, "You know I am just like these boxes, no one knows about them in here. I mean, yes I am new."

The shady man moved on, while Alex did what he was doing. He kept those boxes one by one in each of the cars. He sneaked out slowly without getting anybody's attention. After all the last thing Alex could have wanted was to be shipped along with these cars to Middle East. Yes that is where it was headed to, the land of living hell for people like Alex. I mean seriously which country cuts off your thing for having sex with someone who is not your wife. It was hell.

Alex scrolled down his camera, and there it was pictures of all the forged papers. Rubin was so going to hate this, and Police was so going to love this. Alex thought, it was better that Rubin had stayed away from Audrey. Wait was this all becoming a fight for Audrey. Nah, Alex loved his freedom and just wanted to free again, hitting the clubs, meeting hot women, and taking them to hotel, no either his place or her place. This was all for now with Larry.

Now Alex had shifted his attention to Alina. Oh, and she deserved all the attention of men, she really did, though didn't got much as men like Alex were rare in her life. Alina had a similar living conditions like Christie. Alina too lived in her office, i mean the hotel was her office and she had a suite assigned to her by Rubin. Most of her day was occupied with operations of Rubin's hotels, Bars, and Restaurants. While whenever she got a little free from it, she did the other dirty works of Rubin. As Layla had told Alex, Alina was a micro criminal. I mean she would never thurst a knife in some man or woman, but maybe could give him or her a poisoned coffee. You will never find a single speck of cocaine in her belongings or even in her suite or even in front of her, but then she would close her eyes whenever peddlers supplied drugs in Rubin's clubs.

The woman inside her was still there, unlike Christie who always moaned of her missing soap, and not for once would admit that it was damn good French soap to be stolen. Today Alina had visited a huge hall popular for its charity event and Alex had followed her. Inside she was talking with few people while Alina's helpers were bringing in briefcases from her car. Someone tapped Alex from behind.

The man said, "Hey what are you doing here? The place is closed."

Alex said, "Oh, I didn't knew that. By the way what are you doing here, if the place is closed?"

The man sighed, "I work here, mister. And there is some serious business going on here."

Alex patted on his back, "So that means, it is business hours. So I can be here. Oh there is the café. Do you need a cup, cause I am getting one for myself."

The man felt puzzled, and didn't mind but carried on. Alex went to the café, while Alina had already finished her discussion and started moving out. Alex damned himself, but wait if Alina is gone and so are her conversation, maybe Alex could get in and see what was in those briefcases. Alex took the alley and approached them from the same door Alina had exited. He made himself looked if he was in rush. He approached the men from the hall.

Alex said, "Wait, I think they were meant to be 17, but we have given you 18. So that means 1 more, and our boss doesn't likes a thing less or a thing more. Okay what if it didn't matter if they were 17 or 18, and the things were no less or no more. Wait, we will have to check. Please open them."

Their chief said, "Excuse me, who are you?"

Alex laughed, "Seriously, you don't do prayers before meals. I am your god, the god that brings business to your house, and breads to your table. Come on ask him, I am with Alina."

Alex pointed to the same man who had questioned him, and he nodded, while the chief said, "Okay, thanks for the bread. By the way there is no need to bring god in between, as you are with Alina, here it is."

Good god, what was this. Alex stood there for a moment, awestruck, as he never seen that many gems and diamonds together. Yes all these briefcases were filled with precious gems, the same gems that were liked more than Alex by any of his past girlfriends. They were the one that were most sought by women, not Alex. He did felt a little bit of jealousy, but then started counting them, and taking pictures of it. To this the chief blocked his camera.

The chief said, "Hey what are you doing? For god sake let these stolen bounties be sold first."

Alex stammered, "Oh they are not Facebook, buddy. It is for Alina, to re check everything."

Alex continued clicking their pictures, and bonus he got with a picture of list of buyers. This was all in. Alex left with air in his chest and evidences in his camera. Seriously, this Rubin was everything a criminal would want to be, everything an ideal criminal of the century would want to be. Still he was waking free, while Alex had entire city Police after him. For a minute Alex thought of stealing one of those gems and proposing Alina, God damn she was all worth it. Honestly speaking if someone after Mia had touched the chords of his pants, it was Alina. In fact Alex was enjoying following Alina. He would get to see her moves, her elegance, and her nastiness. Come on, if a man does crime, it is crime, but for women it is little nasty kind of thing, as Alex thought.

Alex thought that these gems must have been near to 5 or 6 million dollars. That was some money, no, that was huge money. The funny part was that Rubin was organizing a charity event for auction of these gems. This way he wouldn't come under Police scanner, and also get more than average bids for these stones. He was damn smart, but not enough for a First Division Buffalo graduate. Alex followed Alina, while she met most of the staff from different hotels of Rubin. In between she also calmed an irate customer over some housekeeping issue. Alex was just awed by her skills, on how good a house keeper she was, ah house maker, ah the runner of errands. Then Alina met with a suited man, similar to the one he had seen in the port. It appeared Alina was in mid of some serious business.

Alina said, "I hope the papers are ready. Because we just got this day, to make millions."

The suited man said, "Don't worry, he won't doubt us a bit."

Then a car stopped and a rich looking man stepped down. Alina said, "Ah. Mr. Dennis. I hope the ride was comfortable."

The rich man said, "Well, honestly I wouldn't have mind bumps, if you were alongside."

Alina smiled, "Oh. I am glad to know that you like bumps. So, I will be more careful while showing you around the hotel. Ah, your hotel. Soon to be."

Alex watched them enter the hotel Raffles. Wait, Hotel Raffles was not of Rubin, as per the research work of Audrey and all the Google search Alex had done. Something was fishy, in fact everything was fishy. That suited man gave Alina the forged papers. Alex saw Mr. Dennis been headed to the administrative office of Hotel, but Alina stopped him and said, 'Oh, the owner doesn't sits here.'. It was obvious that Alina was selling somebody else's hotel to this Mr. Dennis who liked bumps, by making it appear as one of the property of Rubin. Great, I mean, if this Rubin wasn't stopped, then in next decade the city of Angelano be put on sale on ebay. Alex went inside the admin office.

Alex said, "The question may seem odd, but does this hotel by anyway belong to Rubin Maestro."

The admin guy said, "The answer to it will also appear odd. Fuck off."

Seriously, did Alex just threw a hand grenade or a question to this admin guy. Then a man listening to them while on a distant chair approached him and said, "Ah, don't be upset. It's just that Rubin has bad eyes on this hotel. So he is an enemy, and our Admin manager doesn't likes him. So he threw the grenade. You thought right."

This was an extreme that Alex hadn't even thought of. Can't just a man, okay a criminal man sell his own one of dozen hotels and not actually make fool of a bump loving man by selling hotel of a competitor which the man doesn't even own. If this news came out, then probably all the hotel owners of Angelano would come down at Rubin. This was some news, ah this was great news. But there was more to it for sure. The day hadn't ended, and Alina must have got something more special for Alex. But wait, it had been hours since Dennis and Alina were inside the hotel. Then they came out, and Alina kissed cheek to cheek with Dennis, while it felt Dennis has had lots of bump during his tour. Seriously, Alex felt like killing Dennis, for having kissed and polluted Alina. But maybe, Dennis was an older self of Alex who still liked women. Ah, it wasn't worth it,

Alex thought and kept following Alina. She stopped at city's one of most popular record studio, and met with his manager. What they talked, Alex couldn't, but probably she came here hiring musicians for gigs at Rubin's clubs. But seriously, with Rubin around, it could also have been piracy of music CD racket. Alex followed her, and then she stopped at the back of one of Rubin's hotel. There were lines and crowd of teenagers. She met with a man who seem to have assured her that everything was fine. Then a teen walked off with two bottles of Vodka. That was normal, wait he had pimples, and this was Rubin, so it had to selling liquor to under age teens. Good God, what else was left. Alex approached a boy buying liquor.

Alex said, "Hey, how old are you?"

The boy said, "Enough to empty this bottle, and more than enough to shove the empty bottle in you back."

Alex confronted him, "Ah, you know that is the problem of your generation. You just can't see through beyond that back. I mean behind the scene. Do you know why Govt. puts an age restriction on liquor consumption?"

The boy said, "I don't know. I will have to ask the government."

Alex whiffed, "Don't bring in Govt. in between. You know what, when an underage man drinks liquor, his thing stops working. You know what thing I am talking about. The same thing you want to use when you are drunk with a woman. And these people selling liquor are stopping you to become a man."

The boy said, "Oh my god, I just realized that I am losing my interest in sex. What do I do."

Alex took out his camera, "Let's make a video of exposing these people. You just testify their illegal business."

The boy said, "Wait, but what will I get out of this video. My interest of sex has died."

Alex gulped, "Okay what about I will buy you five bottles of vodka for you for free".

The boy said, "But that would then just cremate my interest."

Alex said, "Ah that is out of goodwill, and things done in goodwill do no harm. Come on lets shoot."

The boy repeated, "Rubin Maestro you prick, you are cheater to every under age man of Angelano. You sell us illegal liquor, yes you see this stash I have bought from your illegal store. You make us drink in age when we are supposed to be playboys, ah playing boys. I curse you that your kids will be born in hangover. You prick."

The boy had got little emotional, but the damage was done. With all these Alex had got his chance to make

Rubin confess that he did those crimes which Alex was blamed for.

~~

Chapter 13

The plan was simple, expose Rubin, get him arrested and make him confess about the crimes he did. Of all the crimes he did if proven, he would easily admit that he also killed Audrey, Terry, and of course the Eddie bank transfer was a proof that Alex already had. But wait, he couldn't have disclosed that he actually hacked the Bank of Bahamas, especially in court of law, but then once when Police had confiscated all assets of Rubin, they would also get hands on his bank accounts, hence the Eddie truth would come out sooner or later. All the efforts of hiding in hats, caps, and long overcoats while chasing Alina and Larry had paid off. Seriously Alex had never dressed so consciously even before hitting girls, but wait that didn't mean Alex wasn't serious about girls. The only thing that Alex feared was if Rubin would buy out people in Govt. as Police was corrupt, so his best chance was Media, to let all the people of Angelano know what the owner of their favorite hotel actually did. Alex called Edward.

Alex said, "Guess what I have found the attempted murderer of Joe Winslow, and the drug Lord of Angelano. The same man behind the death of Audrey, and Terry, for now it might sound like me, but I am going to change it. And I need your help."

Edward said, "I am all yours except, if you want to expose somebody else on National TV."

Alex said, "Come on, we are talking about Rubin Maestro. The guy is already favorite of Media channels. Reporters hate him, and it will be the last story on him."

Edward snapped back, "For God sake Alex, this Rubin has filed three lawsuits against city's biggest media houses. Of all the fear Reporters have, I am sure this fourth lawsuit will be the last one. Alex, don't take it personally. I mean me saying a no. It is just because the other guy is Rubin, and he is not fraction of decent like Jody."

Alex hanged up. Deep down Alex knew that especially after the Jody incident, no other Media house would listen to him, and especially running a story against Rubin. But then what were these evidences for. Alex wasn't going to frame these in some shack house of Bahamas spending a life as a fugitive of Angelano. And No way, Alex was going to Jail for what he didn't do. Keep trying was the best bet Alex could make. Alex called other of his few Media friends. Few were even surprised to hear from him, while others suggested that he should surrender, and some said that they can't talk to a fugitive or they would come under Police scanner. Seriously how would Police know with whom Alex was talking with on a new phone. Everybody was deserting him, and he so felt like a criminal.

Criminal, wait, there was one man who could have helped Alex. He was popular, he was sturdy, and he was honest. But Alex's history with him wasn't at its best. But only if Alex was able to convince him, he was the best man that could have pulled Alex out from this mess. Yes it was Detective Joe Winslow. But would Joe even talk with him after Eddie tried murdering him. Anyways, Joe was the only person in the city who must have been thinking about Alex. Seriously, while Alex wanted to be remembered for great nights, this man Joe must be thinking about Alex spending nights in Prison. Alex collected all the evidences and emailed him. He waited for few minutes, and made a call to Joe.

Alex said, "Today is your lucky day, to get hands on your two favorite people. One whom you can convict but can't catch, and two whom you can catch but can't convict. This is Alex, and I am giving you the biggest criminal of Angelano, Rubin Maestro. Detective I have evidences against him, check your mailbox."

Joe said, "Two people at a time. I hope you aren't planning to kill me with happiness."

Alex said, "Detective trust me, that Eddie thing was a setup, and I have proof that Rubin gave Eddie that money to kill you. I mean why would I hire a hit man, when I myself am good at hitting, but only women. I am not much into men. Now i want you to arrest Rubin with these evidences, and he will confess. I bet that."

Jody while checking his mailbox said, "So you admit you are into women. I think Audrey was a woman too."

Alex said, "Yeah she was, but right now you will find these evidences more interesting."

Jody laughed, "These pictures of Larry exchanging brown packets don't indicate that there is brown sugar in them. And don't tell me that one picture of that white block is cocaine, as the defense could also prove it a beauty soap bar. Oh these retail mart papers. Do you even know to whom this retail mart belonged to? It is the second time it is been illegally seized. These people on your side are themselves thugs and their testimony counts nothing. And wait, these forged papers of stolen cars. Do you think you can prove anything? No. They are not fake damn it, the transport officer had made a new originals for these cars, and I know he is corrupt, but we won't be able to prove anything. Alex you are wasting your time, everybody knows Rubin is dirty. Just think about yourself".

Alex said, "Come on Detective, you can't do this. I mean you can. If you can convict me with traces of sperm on a bed sheet, you can sure get Rubin his share of Karma with this. There is more, don't be so quick."

Jody sniffed, "Oh these diamonds, you think they are stolen. But how will you prove it with these pictures. Don't you think he must have already altered, and re shaped them? Oh then there is sale of Hotel Raffles. Do you know that Rubin also has a Real Estate business which might not be legitimate, but this charge will cost him a fine of couple of grands. And this teenager testifying against Rubin, is no use. For god sake he is drunk."

Alex said, "You know what detective, you have made up your mind that I killed Audrey."

Jody snapped, "So, what else do you expect me to do. I wasn't the one found in a room with dead body."

Jody continued, "Listen Alex, don't act stupid. You are not a detective, in fact you are an alleged criminal now. Surrender, and let Police do their Job. I promise, I will listen to all your arguments. But do not make it tough for us."

Alex hanged up the phone. Seriously, after following Larry and Alina for days this was what he got. In fact Alex didn't even fantasized a bit of Alina, only because these evidences were more important to him. Alex thought, maybe Joe was right, these evidences were not strong enough. A bar soap also looked like packed cocaine. Who knew, if Christie would come up and testify that these white packets were her soap, and allege Alex of being mentally sick. Seriously those men from Mart appeared to be so nice, and this was their reality. Maybe that father cum peddler was right, there was no going against Rubin. For a minute it appeared to Alex, if Joe was sold out to Rubin. He didn't even listen a bit to what Alex had to say. Seriously, even the Police knew that Transport officer was corrupt, and they also knew that they could do nothing about that. This Police also knew that Rubin had an illegitimate Real Estate business, but they would only put a fine on him.

I mean what world, Alex had been living in. Such a Police was no good, and could never get him justice. Was this the fate written for Alex to rot in prison. Of course not! But now all these evidences made no sense, Alex had to do something bigger, But what? Detective Joe Winslow was right about one thing, Alex was not a detective, he was marketer, a damn good marketer, who always had out of the box ideas, most creative pitches, but of all he never had known Police work. But catching Rubin was also crucial to his freedom. Alex ran his mind in all directions he could. For Alex his speech on 'Marketing, as it should be' was favorite, and whenever he felt low and insignificant, he would remember the claps that followed his speech. Alex thought, wait, why to become someone else to bring down a man like Rubin. Alex was what he was, and he was enough to bring down Rubin and make him confess. This was not over yet. He quickly took out his phone and called Nathan.

Alex said, "Hey, I don't care if you are cooking muffins with Julia, or tossing a pizza on her booty. What I know is, that I need your help, and you are going to do this for me."

Nathan said, "Whoa Alex, it sounds you are in deeper shit. And hey, the thing between me and Julia is over. Yeah, she is dating a freaking immigrant from Milan who speaks Italian, wears Italian, eats Italian, and I think they just went on a holiday to sleep in Italian. I mean sleep in Italy. Anyways how can I help."

Alex said, "I told you about Rubin, and Alina right. I need you to get Office access card of Alina for me to break in."

Nathan said, "Hey Alex, I know it might sound as I am sad because Julia left. But I still love my life."

Alex said, "Hey, Alina would not even know that you stole it. You just have to keep her busy."

Nathan said, "Come on Alex, you kidnapped the daughter of Police Commissioner. Can't you do this?"

Alex snapped back, "For god sake Nathan, Alina handles Human resources for Rubin. You know how they are, like our HR of High Rise. She even knew who liked hot dogs, and who liked bare sausages. Come on, Alina will recognize me in a second, after all those prime time news shows. I can't face her."

Nathan said, "And what will happen when she knows I did it. I will be gone Alex. They are not Police, they are criminals. They will not try to catch me, but they will kill me."

Alex said, "Trust me Nathan, in all of this plot, you are just a sidekick. No one will know you."

Nathan snapped back, "So i will always be a sidekick haan. Anyways, just don't screw this up."

The plan was set and so were the people who were going to pull it. Nathan had reached the Hotel All Stars, it was the same hotel where Rubin had his headquarters. It was the same hotel where Alina had her company suite. The plan looked simple, but wasn't that easy. Nathan today was going to pretend and act like if he was an Art dealer. Well he wasn't good at acting, or else he too could have pretended he knew everything about Italy by telling a story or two about Julius Caesar. But one thing that was going to work well was that Nathan knew a lot about arts. HE could have easily pulled off a discussion with anyone about who was mightier, Michelangelo or Picasso.

Tonight Nathan had to meet Alina, and draw her to a conversation on how they could do business together. While talking he just had to made sure that Alina left the table twice. First for Alex to steal that access card from her purse, and second for Alex to put back that access card in her purse, but in between these two times Alex had to break inside Rubin's headquarters and do his thing. Of all these days that Alex was following Alina, he had noticed that she went down the hotel to the restaurant to have dinner on every consecutive days, while on rest of the days she had dinner room serviced in her apartment.

Tonight was that consecutive day, and Alex was praying hard that she came down. After having gone with evidences to Media and Detective Joe Winslow, this was his only window to make Rubin confess of his crimes. But seriously, this was also the first time Alex was stealing something from women, well mostly he only borrowed 'The Protection Thing', but tonight he had to take a step further. They saw Alina coming, while Nathan panicked. Alex patted his back.

Alex said, "Come on man, you can do this. See how sexy she is. Think of me when I hit women to take them to beds, but for you, it is just going to be till the dinner table."

Nathan said, "The last thing I will do is think of you, or seriously it is going to end in a bed, death bed."

Alina stopped to start a conversation with the restaurant manager. They were talking about the crowd getting lesser on weekends. A waiter approached Alina, and she told him to bring the regulars. She was looking calm, and she was looking everything a man would want. But Nathan didn't want her tonight, not because he was not a man, but a friend to Alex first. Nathan stopped by side of Alina, and with surprise got headed towards her.

Nathan said, "Ah. Ah. You are Alina, from Priceless Charities. What a pleasant surprise."

Alina smiled, "I am sorry but I don't recall you. By the way I am not from Priceless Charities, but yes we do get our auctions organized by them."

Nathan said, "Of course that is where I saw this priceless smile before. Do you know, I bought a diamond ring from your auction, to propose to my girlfriend! That was the best cut diamond I had ever seen, and my girlfriend was so happy to have it, and flaunts it till this date."

Alina said, "Of course she will. Proposal rings are special, and even special when it comes from our house."

Nathan said, "Oh yes, but she even flaunts it after we broke up. She thinks Vinci is good but not the greatest, because he can't make a woman feel happy and be obvious about it, and that he was a bastard. I found it outrageous listening to an insult of a God like figure to me. So we broke up, but she still has the ring."

Alina said, "Oh didn't knew that. I mean that you broke up. So what brings you here?"

They both have now seated on a table while Alina had ordered him a steak. Nathan said, "I am an arts dealer. Though I don't have hands on work of Monet, or Vermeer or Vincent Van Gough, but I do have some great all time classics, and plus I also deal in some big time duplicates of popular works. I was in Angelano to meet another dealer who could arrange an auction for works I have procured. But it didn't went well."

Alina bent forward, "Oh if you don't mind, tell me. My boss would love to enter this business."

Nathan said, "Don't get me wrong, but duplicate works like Bacchus, Annunciation, Anxiety sell like hot cakes, because buyers often flaunt them as originals as no one as heard of them."

Alina raised her brows, "Tell me more, it sounds like good business."

Meanwhile Nathan waved his hands across the table to pick that Salad bowl and spilled the glass of wine of Alina's dress. She whiffed and stood up, while Nathan said, "I am so sorry. I just didn't."

Alina interrupted, "Ah, its okay. I have many dresses like these. You just stay here, I will be back."

Alex who was watching them over, reached their table and sat in Alina's place with slightly checking her purse. Yeah, he got it. He patted Nathan and strode towards the lift. Half of the plan had worked. Now rest was a quick ride in elevator to the top of hotel to reach Rubin's headquarters. Alex hurried and did his best to stay out of attention. The hallway was dark, and this time it was different. He was breaking into a criminal's place, who knew if a gunman was sitting in a dark corner inside ready to shoot trespassers.

This time if Alex got caught, he wouldn't go to jail, but to graveyard, with Nathan mourn on his grave, after all friends were for that. Alex watched his steps and peeped through the glass door while the office was empty. He swiped the access card and rushed towards the marketing department. Yes it was where he was going to find the next weapon to bring down Rubin. He opened the system, and started checking it. It took few minutes, while Alex kept browsing. He smiled, and there it was what he was seeking, the destruction of Rubin was right in front of him. He looked around, but the camera's were off. In fact Rubin was so confident that he had installed virtually no cameras in his office thinking nobody got that balls to break into his office.

But this time not just balls, but entire man with a loose pant was on brink of destroying him. Alex held to his nerves and clicked the button. He rushed back to see that Nathan and Alina had almost become friends. Seriously, first Julia and then Alina.. What was wrong with women of Angelano. Nathan saw Alex's thumbs going up.

Nathan said, "Hey. Criminals too are people, and I am a people's man. Have you heard about Caravaggio? In 16th century he used to carry a sword without permit, he attacked many with the same sword, he hired assassins to kill Giovanni, he threw a plate of artichokes on a waiter's face, he went to prison for throwing stones at policemen, he injured himself by falling on his own sword. Ha. But you know he was a damn good painter. His works like Judith Beheading Holofernes are still the best masterpieces around."

Alina couldn't stop smiling and said, "You would at least sell one painting of Caravaggio to my boss."

Nathan said, "Ah, isn't is a strange world we live in. The mighty Raphael died because of having too much of sex, just to keep his artistic blend alive. That didn't made him a pervert. We know him as greatest artist of all time."

Nathan again waved his hand to spill the bottle on Alina, but she got hold of it and said, "Caught you."

Nathan and Alex both got panicked, while Alina rose and said, "See you tomorrow Nathan. Boss will love to meet you. And I am sure you have a story to tell him. I mean stories like these."

Both had got the color of their face wiped. Alina started walking towards the door but she had forgotten her purse. Alex rushed and slid the access card in it, while Nathan followed her and patted on her back.

Nathan said, "You forgot your purse. Keep it, you are going to need it later." Alina smiled and moved on.

~~

Chapter 14

This wasn't any other night, it was a night to be remembered. Tonight Rubin was about to face his worst of nightmares, and Police was about to have their day. Alina had got back to her hotel suite, thinking of how this new art dealer could bring in Millions for Rubin. While she thought that Rubin would so happy with her, she was unaware that she had just help Alex dig his grave. Nathan was still little scared because of all the stories he had told, he didn't wanted to become one. While the rest of town had gone back to sleep, Alex was all vigilant, and had parked his car just outside Rubin's house. I mean seriously after having snatched Alex's breath, how could Alex have let Rubin have a sound sleep.

On nights when Alex was supposed to hitting on women like Alina, he was actually stealing stuff from her purse. This is what Alex considered a nightmare coming true. A woman like Alina with bounty of beauty had become Alex's enemy, and all this was because of Rubin. He was the man responsible for Alex breaking into Alina's office and not her suite. Alex thought of Audrey, and all that couldn't happen because this Rubin had come in between. Having an account in Bank of Bahamas didn't made Rubin invincible, because he didn't knew that Alex always like exploring the exotica.

Tonight was the day, when Journalists were going to have their piece of Rubin, by all means. I mean seriously what business owner does harm to their customer, a retarded businessman, just like Rubin. Of course Alex wasn't his customer of cocaine, but it was his acts of hitting on women that still kept Floor on Fire a hip place. There was one thing that Alex was lamenting on, that how come he didn't notice that owner of that dirty club could be the drug lord and killer of Audrey. But it was all okay, as now he was in the place. Alex's phone rang, and it was Nathan.

Nathan said, "Hey did it worked? Because I am little scared of a SUV parked outside my house."

Alex said, "It has to work, I know these people. And by the way, that SUV parked is not because of you meeting with Alina, but because you are a miser and haven't put a NO Parking Board on your fence."

Nathan said, "Oh so now I am a miser, but I wasn't when I paid for that bottle of wine for Alina."

Alex said, "Oh that was because you were trying on her. I know you Nathan, what you saw in those dresses of Milan of Julia, and god it was in your eyes on how badly you wanted to get rid of them. You know what, I did you a favor by introducing to Alina. You can thank me later, once you paint her with your thing. Hey wait, I think it's working."

Alex hanged up the phone, while a sports car dropped by Rubin's house and a man wearing a hoodie approached the gate. The man in hoodie talked with the watchman and waited. In another few minutes, few more people dropped by Rubin's house, they too exchanged words with watchman and waited. It kept repeating, and soon it was hoard of people outside Rubin's house. Alex couldn't help but smile. The people outside Rubin's house were getting restless and were agitating. Few of Rubin's men came out from his house to calm them down, while the crowd kept increasing. Alex had eyes set on the glass wall of Rubin's room. Soon it lit up with light. There were men inside his room, trying to wake up Rubin who was few glasses of Whisky down. Then the glass door of his room opened, and there he was the man behind half of the crimes of Angelano peeping out at the crowd. For a minute Alex thought that Rubin was also looking at his car, and maybe his face too. But that was obvious, Rubin was looking at every car parked outside his house. It was just too much chaos for a night. Rubin went back.

Rubin said, "Hey call our men, and give them what they need. Just get rid of this crowd."

Meanwhile Alex texted Joe Winslow, "Detective, something big is happening at Rubin's house. This is your chance, so come down with all the force you got. Your not so favorite, Alex."

With passing of every minute, the crowd at Rubin's house kept increasing. To control them, Rubin's men were now at the house gate with arms in their hands. It has been a while, then few Fords and Chevrolets came by Rubin's house. These cars kept their distance, and then Alex noticed that Detective Joe Winslow got out from one of them. Yes, the Police had arrived. Alex smiled as his plan was working just fine. Seriously, he hadn't been that happy ever before, even on last New Year Eve when he was invited over to a night out by 3 hot girls. Wait, it didn't mean that for Alex happiness wasn't something else than getting laid, but that night those 3 hot girls had drank too much that they slept over the entire night.

For the first time in his life Alex had realized that apart from sleeping with women, nailing your enemies also had a different level of joy. Prior to this day, there was only 'I screw you' in Alex's life, but tonight the mantra had changed to 'You screw me, I screw you'. Rubin had no idea what he had got himself into, especially for tonight. Meanwhile, Detective Joe Winslow and his men had now diffused in the crowd and they were talking with them.

Then few men came in striding into Rubin's house, and after few minutes they came out to distribute few packets to this crowd. Well, not hard to guess, it was cocaine. Detective Joe Winslow had just got his best opportunity to bust Rubin in a live event of drug distribution. In minutes Cop cars with loud sirens had surrounded the crowd. Everybody was taken into custody, while Joe Winslow had Rubin handcuffed in his night suit, been taken to Police headquarters.

Rubin was yelling at Police, 'Hey this wasn't me, somebody is trying to set me up.'.

Joe Winslow murmured to him, 'Yeah you are right and that somebody is Police of Angelano. Now shut up.'.

Alex called Nathan and said, "Guess what, Rubin is arrested. It worked. Hell yes, it worked. Seriously right now I feel like coming to your house and spray paint on that SUV outside, NO Parking. I love you Nathan, wait I also love Alina, because it wouldn't be possible without her."

Nathan said, "Yeah, it's okay. Guess what who was in the SUV. Julia, she had broken up with that Italian guy, and was feeling awkward on how to face me. I will call you tomorrow morning, as she is staying over."

Seriously, what was wrong with Julia, couldn't she be happy with her Italian taste, and have left this moment for Alex to enjoy with another single man. Something was really wrong with women of Angelano. Alex smiled and this moment he felt like one of the greatest marketer of all times. Seriously could marketing get people arrested, hell yes it could. It was not only guns that were dangerous, but marketing too had joined its league. The deadly marketing was something what Alex would call it.

The night when Alex had broken into Rubin's headquarters, he was not just browsing the computer, but finding the email database of Rubin's all VVIP members of his clubs. Alex had known that VVIP members of Rubin's club had access to his drug peddlers, so he took advantage and mass emailed n messaged them that tonight Rubin will be distributing cocaine to all his VVIP members at his house. Alex always believed in marketing and tonight too it worked like a charm.

Police had also found evidence in the crowd's mobile phones with a message from Rubin's office server. In a nutshell, Rubin was totally screwed. Alex had tried all his amateur detective skills, but tonight what worked was his marketing skills. Marketing can never go wrong. After all it was marketing that had given Alex his job, his good pay slip, a name in society, and applauds of appreciation. If Alex hadn't known about these email, and messaging apps, then maybe he still be waiting out of Rubin's house with no crowd to show up. Seriously, his belief in himself just got stronger. The night went on, with Rubin sleeping on concrete seat inside Police Prison cell. The next morning hordes of Policemen were interrogating him.

Rubin yelled, "I don't know who sent these mails and messages. I am being set up."

Joe said, "But sure you do know who was distributing cocaine at your house, of course not your ghost."

Rubin said, "No detective, not at my house, but outside my house. And even my Ghost wouldn't do such a thing."

Another Policeman got a heap of files and threw towards Rubin on the interrogation table. It was the testimony of people from the same crowd that had gathered to take free cocaine. These people had co-operated with Police and admitted that they on previous occasions too had received cocaine from Rubin. Rubin read it, and threw it back towards the policemen. This man didn't give a damn about the testimonies.

Rubin said, "Detective I am a business man, I might not be a very socially responsible one, but yet I am a good businessman. I run clubs, and many of my clubs have these cheap drug peddlers who do dirty business. I can't stop them, its Police Job. And trust me, no one of these witnesses will ever repeat that looking me in my eye."

Joe said, "Oh some of it is true, because these people for sure don't want to share a prison with you."

Rubin said, "I bet that Detective. But no one is going to prison. Though I pity on the desires of Angelano Police, but I can sure allow you to make a statue of me in Angelano Prison. Maybe it will do good for both of us."

Joe didn't asked any further questions, but other Policemen tried their level best to trap Rubin in their legal lawsuits. Meanwhile Rubin's lawyers had applied for bail for not only Rubin but all those people who were caught receiving drugs. This was a masterstroke from Rubin, to keep them on his side, so they didn't do anything against him. But the damage was done. The Judge was too stern, and no way he was letting Rubin go out from this. The Media of Angelano had got all over the news with footage of drug exchange outside Rubin's house. Alex saw one of them saying on TV, 'See this house, this is where you get Free Cocaine in Angelano. Long time alleged criminal Rubin Maestro did it again. He openly messages his VVIP club members to distribute free cocaine. What world we live in. This man is afraid of nothing, and he is marketing his illegal shit. We the people of Angelano need to tell this man that cocaine doesn't comes free , it comes with a cost of conviction.'.

Seriously Alex had smiled to himself and thanked the media for putting that mayonnaise on top. Edward would be so lamenting on the fact that he didn't bought Alex's story. But then whatever happens, happens for good. Well, not everything, especially the murder of Audrey on a night when they could have done a lot. But then something's did happen for good. If those evidences were aired on Media and Rubin would have made them look baseless, then Alex wouldn't be seeing this moment of glory. Very soon his bad days were about to end, as Alex thought. While in city Rubin was talking to his lawyers.

Rubin said, "I pay you the fattest of pay cheques in city. For this day, to keep me locked up in prison. Damn you people. I have 4 best hotels in this city, and right now I am living on this food truck grade porridge. Maybe I should shove that steak you eat in your back, to make you feel the pain."

Alina said, "Rubin there is more bad news. Many of the witnesses have rejected our legal support."

Rubin said, "How come a man who shows up for free cocaine, doesn't accepts a free lawyer. Try harder."

Another lawyer came striding in and said, "Hey Rubin there is good news. The Judge assigned to this case, is ready for a little bribe, but only to get you the bail. He hasn't said anything about the trail, as there is lot of public pressure. But sure we can get you bail in 3 Million Dollars, plus the bail bond."

Rubin rubbed his nose, "Do you want to pay that money from your salary account, Of course not. Then do it."

Judge happily took the bribe, and granted Rubin bail, but this wasn't over. The lawsuit filed against Rubin was getting stronger as witnesses were now coming in front of Media, people, and Government. In fact, a drug abuse NGO had filed another lawsuit on Rubin. His miseries were just getting started. Of all the decades since he has been running illegal businesses, this was the first time that anybody has came this close to bring him down. Rubin feared that it were his enemies. Of course he had enemies, like the Italian Russo family, and the Mexican Martinez family. Rubin thought that it must have been the Russo's, and he even told few of his men to bust these Italians. By the way, the Italian guy, Julia was dating had no connections with Russo's or Martinez's. Rubin was furious and scared as hell. This lawsuit could have been his last stint with law. He was sitting in his office when his club manager came in.

The club manager said, "Boss, 80 percent of our Club members have revoked their membership."

Another manager said, "Boss, footfall in our restaurants have been all time low at 10% of regular."

His Hotel manager said, "I am sorry to break this, but many booking portals have started to boycott us."

Rubin nodded and whiffed, "Great, even I have some news for you. After all this Business Drama, Rubin laid off 90% of his employees. And you know what, you people have just made it into that 90%. Woohoo. This calls for champagne, while we can still afford it. Screw you, you useless fellows. Can't you control this all fiasco."

Rubin's phone rang and he answered. It was Alex, he said, "So how was the trip Rubin. The special trip without intake of Cocaine, I mean it couldn't have got higher than this."

Rubin said, "Oh, the trip was good, but the day is bad, and I fear if I am going to run over you."

Alex said, "Ouch, I felt the hit. Ha, isn't killing your habit, like you wiped Audrey."

Rubin whiffed, "Well it's always a pleasure to show people the stairway to heaven. If you too want a lift, I won't mind. But these are crazy times, as you know some crack head had just set me up to city's biggest drug scandal. So why the hell you don't tell me, who are you, what you want, and why did you do this."

Alex said, "The answer lies within. Ah, I know you are hollow, but I meant in this conversation."

Rubin scratched his beard, "Is it about Audrey, that Journo who died in my hotel."

Alex said, "I was always told that cocaine eats away your brain, but guess what your IQ has just beaten this fact. Yes Rubin, you cunt, you killed Audrey and you made my life hell. Listen very carefully, I am going to bring you down. There will be no stairway to heaven, but hell in a well. Admit it that you killed Audrey and Terry."

Rubin yelled back, "Listen you prick. That journalist is dead, and if this moves even an inch further, you will die too. Just leave me out of this, now you are ruining my business."

Rubin hanged up the phone, while Alex hit his phone back on his head. The bad news was that he had just missed his chance of making Rubin confess to his crimes, but the Good news was that lawsuit filed against Rubin was still on. If not today, then maybe tomorrow Alex would for sure get his due share of justice. But wait, he couldn't have relaxed in some shady hotel in old town of Angelano. He had to make his another move, and get Rubin down on his knees. Yes, he had to do it. For now it didn't mattered to Alex if Julia had come back to Nathan, of course not because Nathan wasn't his good friend, or because Julia was exactly not his type of girl, but more because Alex wanted to be free, free to enter a burger joint without fear of Police or crowd watching him, free to hit as many clubs as possible in a night.

Alex didn't cared Alina shadowing one particular news channel that had ties with Rubin with a long speech of all charity work Rubin has done and was getting paid with a lawsuit. Well honestly, this PR trick was of no use, and clearly Alina wasn't a match as marketer to Alex, yeah with this mass mailing and messaging Alex had those brownie points over her. Alex knew that another attempt of bringing down Rubin via Alina wouldn't be a good move. But there wasn't anything to worry about, as Alex had Larry in the kitty. Alex knew that this time it had to be through Larry. Though Larry would be more conscious, but then he will be more vulnerable too. Alex picked his phone and made a call to Delvin, remember the same real estate agent who had introduced Alex to Lawrence. Well Delvin wasn't a superman but he was good fit for the plan Alex had for Larry.

Delvin said, "Hey man, you are a freaking celebrity now. You are all over the news. Hey, I also know that you got Rubin down. I always thought you were a kid, a fun loving kid, who liked to have fun with girls. But I was wrong, guess now who is the daddy. Yay."

Alex interrupted, "Hey, hey Delvin, I need your help, to get me out of the shit I am in."

Delvin said, "You know what if you had asked for help a month back, I would have hesitated, because you always called me for cable, plumbing issues, but if this is something cool I am in man."

Alex took a breath, "Hey, but you got to know. It is about bringing down Rubin. But you'll be safe."

Delvin said, "Ah, couldn't have gotten better. Listen man this is good for both of us. You will get your freedom and I will earn my muscle in the market. But hey I need something else from you. After we are done, you are going to introduce me to Junior Walter. Cool with that." Both laughed.

~~

Chapter 15

The plan was simple, while Delvin and Alex were completely in. After all those days that Alex had followed Larry, he had noticed that Larry had a bad habit of over drinking. Wait, it wasn't just about over drinking, but Larry was so boastful of himself that he claimed no one could beat him in a drinking competition. Yes, this thin lean looking man was a tanker. Alex thought that this guy Larry sure would've been a bar's sweetheart in his younger days, as no one would compete with him now. Yeah, it had been a while, but everybody knew that alcohol for Larry was like water. So the plan was to get Larry drunk as hell and get the work done. Rubin on the other hand was limiting his hands. He had paused all of his illegal operations for now, as he didn't wanted any other solid evidence to reach courthouse. Larry who on regular days would run about over the city, was now only checking up with Rubin's associate on telephone. Yeah, they were scared, and they didn't wanted anybody to take advantage of that.

Rubin's business was on all time low. In fact some social activists of Angelano had even organized a silent protest in front of Rubin's properties with bold slogans like 'Give our kids back'. Seriously give our kids back, was this some legal wrangle over the custody of kids, as what marketer inside Alex thought. But in the end of the day it had done its work, as even the National Child Right Society had joined these silent protest for all the kids Rubin had drugged. Alex knew what he had to do, but the problem was getting Larry in his range, because Larry hadn't left Rubin's headquarter since the bailout. So Alex was just keeping an eye, holding to his heart that everything was going to be fine again. After all what a drug lord could do of him. Of all the literature, truth always won, but wait, did Rubin read all those literature, ah, it didn't mattered because Alex had. He then saw Larry leaving the building. Alex called Delvin.

Alex said, "Hey the plan is on. I hope you don't have butterflies in your stomach."

Delvin said, "Nah, that place is reserved for booze for tonight. See you there."

Alex followed Larry to those couple of places he went. Seriously this Rubin was a crack head. Having police on your tail, he still was trying to again run the business. I mean seriously, since the day Alex had moved out of that bed with dead body of Audrey, he hadn't had one good night sleep, but this Rubin had already started to get business back rolling. But maybe when days are done, you stop counting it. That sure did applied on Rubin, maybe he knew his days were done now. But seriously how could somebody live with guilt of murder, theft, illegal crimes, seriously. Wait, Alex thought, wasn't he own living in guilt of having slept with that many women and even not having met them again. But that wasn't guilt, it was joy. So probably Rubin too enjoyed doing this. Maybe they weren't very different then. Alex followed Larry back to the hotel, and had called Delvin en route. Larry was walking through the bar at basement towards the lift, when he heard someone say.

The voice came in, "Hey you know what, men of Angelano should start drinking milk. Yeah that's what you can deal with, you sissy boys. Ha."

It piqued Larry's interest, so he stopped to look back, while Delvin continued. "You know when I was born, my mom gave me a bottle of tequila and said don't worry kiddo life will sure give you lemons, and you know what I said, hey mom, life has already given them. Look at the nurse." He laughed.

Another man said, "I don't believe you, this is all crap."

Delvin snapped back, "Yeah I know, because that is what you can take in. Should I add lemons. Ha."

Larry couldn't resist and said, "Trust me boy, you don't want to do this, unless you are prepared to puke for the rest of your life, and that won't taste good."

Delvin looked back at bartender, "Ah, maybe some people should live by their credit card limits. Ain't it mate."

Larry murmured, 'That's it', and he sat just besides Delvin pointing to the bartender to get started. Delvin laughed, while people around had surrounded them, especially the hotel staff that knew how bad a drunkard Larry was. They were now three drinks down, while Larry along with this drinking competition was also checking his phone, and replying to some work messages. Delvin smiled at Alex that sat at back of bar in a hoodie.

Delvin said, "Oh my god, I need to leave, I have to pick my wife from work. Ha, ha, ha. Its okay with me."

Larry chuckled and shut down his phone. He drank three drinks in one go. The competition was getting stiffer, while Delvin was feeling a little obnoxious about everything. Well, for those who didn't knew, Alex hadn't told Delvin about the bad drinking habit of Larry, so Alex had actually tricked them both in one go. I mean seriously, few more drinks, and Delvin would for sure start to feel pukish. But then few forces in life were way too strong to be overcome by little pegs of tequila, For starters the fatal attraction of Junior Walter. Alex and Delvin didn't knew this girl as Junior Walter just because she was daughter to Mr. Walter, but she had earned her title, by wearing skirts shorter than Mr. Walters half pants. Well for now, Larry had gone into his full drinking mode, and he was drinking least 3 shots for Delvin's one. Delvin looked back at Alex, gesturing if the game was done now.

Larry turned to bartender and said, "I forgot my card, so you can keep the change and drinks too."

Delvin snapped back, "Oh no, no, no. You will now have a drink on my coffin. Gimme more."

Larry laughed loud, and they drank. In between Larry looked a couple of times at Delvin, who had totally lost it to an extent that he was keeping himself awake by sprinkling shots on his face. But just like his boss, Larry kept his honor by drinking more and more, while at back of the bar, something huge was waiting for Larry. The men were cheering Larry, but their sounds couldn't supersede every time Larry asked for another drink. The time has come, no not to announce the winner as the night had just started, but to pee. So Larry left his chair to head to washroom. Delvin saw this and stood up dialing some number on his phone.

Delvin yelled, "Oh so you too wanna compete with me. Hey hold the drinks I am coming."

Delvin exited, while another man said, "Ah, he is so full of crap that too without lemons."

Alex knew what exactly was going to happen next. Larry came in and laughed to see Delvin gone. Larry moved to another table and got himself another bottle of vodka. This was what Alex knew, that Larry would continue to drink. Larry was making himself drink, while Alex got himself seated opposite to him.

Larry said, "You know what, I can do this all night. You want to make a bet."

Larry was pretty much drunk, so he couldn't recognize Alex. Alex said, "Nah, but I would like to bet on this bar, maybe on this hotel, maybe on Rubin."

Larry chuckled, "What, wait, Rubin doesn't plays these kind of games. He has other toys."

Alex said, "Yeah I know, and I also know that business is doing bad."

Larry said, "Ah, I think I am little drunk. And when I am drunk, I don't see straight, and as of now I also can't see where this is going. So I won't mind a hand, I mean your hand, to explain me that what exactly do you want. Ah, if it is the drinks, the bar is all yours, cause tonight I won't stop anybody drinking."

Alex said sharply, "I want to buy this hotel."

Larry took a deep breath. No matter how drunk he was, but he was always a loyal and well-wisher of Rubin. If Rubin was here, and drunk too, to not recognize Alex, still Rubin would have said F OFF to Alex. But Larry knew how money worked, and a buyer coming in at this point of time was like god send. The hotel was doing bad, and in no near future it had possibility of recovering especially till it was owned by Rubin, as Larry knew. So he shook hands with Alex and they talked. Alcohol could make you lose your focus, but never the money. It was so apt, and Larry hadn't been happier. Larry even showed him few papers he had in his briefcase, and exchanged few account numbers. The drinking game was eventually won by Larry, and he had scored good in it. What he didn't knew was that Rubin was going to lose bad time. It was true, that Karma was a bitch, and now it was about to bite back Rubin.

Alex left Larry lying on the restaurant table, who was later carried to a suite by the hotel people. The man had his drinks, and now the man was having his night. This night Larry was sleeping like a monster, with no clue if he ever had to even wake up, he had won a game of drinks, and also proposed selling his hotel to a buyer who was Alex. On the other hand, Alex was not able to seep even for a second. All night he was hung up on phone, talking to an old friend. With only three to four grands in hand he was now looking to buy a property of Rubin. Wait, what was it, some enemy empathy, well definitely not, he had some other plans. On the extreme other hand, there was another person who tried very hard to sleep, but had a rough night because of constant messages he received, it was Rubin. Rubin was irritated and furious, while the next morning he walked up to his office where Larry sat sipping black coffee.

Rubin said, "Hey Larry, I don't know why but the entire last night I have been receiving money to my few accounts. Would you take a look, to what is happening?"

Larry said with lit up face, "I got it, you know last night I met a buyer, who is interested in this hotel."

Rubin said, "Are you sure, he was buyer and not a beggar. Just look at it."

Rubin gave Larry his mobile phone, which had account transfers of 1 dollar, 2 dollars, 5 Dollars, up till maximum of 10 dollars, and there were 100's of these transfers. Larry felt confused, and couldn't understand, on why these account transfers were made. It didn't made sense, in fact with such amount that buyer last night would not even get a tea in this hotel, in fact forget about tea, he won't be able to pee with this amount. Larry's head was paining, especially with the yelling his wife gave him this morning. Maybe it was enough of drinking games.

Rubin said, "You know what, just call the bank and reverse these transactions, even if it takes more than this money to reverse it. No way I am taking that money. I mean it's not even qualified to be called money."

A man came striding in their office and panted. He said, "Boss, we have got a situation. There are dozens of men, well some huge men, asking when will the winner be announced, its already time, as they are saying."

Rubin said, "What the F. What winner will announced, tell them to go away if they don't want to lose, their life."

Rubin laughed and continued, "Wait, Larry, last night you played that drinking game. Yes or No?"

Larry exhaled, while huge noises started coming in from the alley outside their office. Larry peeped out to see, that some mountain biker kind of men, along with burger stuffed kind of men, along with truck drivers kind of men, and more kind of men, along with many red haired women, were creating ruckus in Rubin's office. They were yelling, and they were shouting, some were annoyed, some were abusing, the scene wasn't very good. Then a bunch of Police officers came striding in. They talked with those men, to calm them and straight got headed to Rubin's office. Larry didn't felt very great and murmured, Shit. The Police men entered.

The Police Officer said, "Mr. Rubin, you are under arrest. You have all rights to stay silent."

Rubin interrupted, "F You, I will not stay silent, what is this about, ain't your judge got the bail money."

The Police Officer folded his hands and said, "Yes he got it. But this arrest is for a different case. You are being charged with running an illegal Lottery business in city of Angelano. You are being charged for running Lottery Scam and cheating people with their money. Now your hands where I can put the cuffs."

Rubin yelled, "Are you serious. Well Lottery business sounds good, but I have heard it for first time."

The damage was done, Police was again taking Rubin into custody. A fresh lawsuit was filed against him. By the way, it was Alex that had called the Police with statements of these poor men n women who were hoping to win a lottery. Let's go back in time a bit. Last night, when Alex sat with Larry, he told Larry that he would buy the hotel, even if the entire house keeping staff was male, ah, anyways Alex wasn't going to buy it, but he proposed. So Larry trying to be a faithful man of Rubin, instantly gave Alex a copy of Property papers that he always carried in his briefcase. Alex asked, if Larry could give him the account numbers of Rubin, he would send in token money. Larry of course gave Alex the numbers.

This is what they both knew, but what Larry didn't knew was that Alex went back to Marvin, and made Marvin create a micro site of Online Lottery business. It barely took Marvin a couple of hours to do so, and Alex made Marvin attach Rubin's account numbers for transaction of every Lottery ticket purchased. To make the website genuine and trap Rubin forever, he attached the property papers of that hotel on the website as office registered address. Marvin did rest of the damage by promoting that website on dark web. Now all these people had purchased lottery tickets, while money got transferred to Rubin, who couldn't sleep the other night because of messages. Seriously, Marketing always worked, if you reached out to right people.

Now Angelano PD had written complaints of all these Lottery buyers accusing Rubin of fraud, plus lottery was illegal in Angelano. I mean seriously, Alex made Rubin looked like a high school girl on periods, with shame and embarrassment attached. An ex-employee of High Rise

Marketing was on verge of destroying the biggest illegal businessman of Angelano, if someone believed that something is just not possible. Plus Alex did this without even raising a gun. Well his gun was having a bad time, the other gun who would only get solace in one of Rubin's clubs. While in Police HQ, Detective Joe Winslow was having his life time days by interrogating Rubin.

Rubin said, "Detective I am being set up. Yes, it is him, that boy Alex. Honestly speaking, once I did thought about Lottery business, but I didn't do it, because its illegal, and i am bad with luck."

Joe said, "Oh you sure are bad in luck, I bet that. I mean two days, two lawsuits."

Rubin said, "Detective think, why would I do this, that too for thousand dollars. Come on, I have just paid 1 million dollar as bail bond. Do you think I am crazy to do this."

Joe said, "I wish you would have earned more money in Lottery, because you are so going to need it."

Other Police officers kept interrogating him, while Rubin had even no clue on how to even lie to them, because he didn't know a thing about this. The Media of Angelano had truly got crazy over Rubin's row.

The same Judge who had taken bribe from Rubin was giving statements like, 'He thinks he can mock the judicial power of this country, not till I am alive'. The media on other hand was lashing out their worst with statements like, 'This man kills our kids, and bankrupts their dad's, Enough of you Rubin'. Everywhere it was Rubin, Rubin, and Rubin. This time he was going to have it from law, and there was no escaping. On a lighter note, Alex was also happy that all the attention of police on him was now diverted to Rubin. Alex was just one step away from getting Rubin's confession. Larry while hitting his head in office had now remembered that it was Alex that night, while in conversation with Alina who told him about the arts dealer she met. So, now apart from getting Rubin's confession, Alex also had to save his back from these hardened criminals. But seriously, if one were to ask on who would be most sad on closure of Rubin's businesses, it would be Alex, after all Floor on Fire would also get shut. It was not just this, Alex would also be cursed by many virgins who regarded Floor on Fire as their temple.

But then having a life was better than having pants down. Seriously, if all the Media had now known that all of this was done by Alex, he would for sure become an overnight hero, but then time wasn't right, first he had to prove himself innocent. Meanwhile in Police headquarters, Joe Winslow had got his brows raised. He had doubted that Alex wouldn't be hiding quietly, but all of this done by Alex came to him as a shock. He called the same policeman that had spotted him in the hotel earlier, but was fooled by bunch of hippies.

Joe said, "It isn't over yet, we still have Alex to catch. Remember he is still a criminal."

The Police officer said, "I know detective, but isn't he also a hero, I mean he got us Rubin."

Joe snapped back, "You know what is the weakest trait of a Police man, to trust a criminal. He can fool Rubin, but not me. You might think that he didn't killed Audrey. But not the people, and remember that girl has died, and someone has to deal with that fact. This time, you spot him, take him in, or rather take him out."

~~

Chapter 16

Audrey didn't die for nothing. She had believed that the city of Angelano needed to be free of drugs and free of people like Rubin. The last person with whom she shared this vision was Alex, and it was now that Alex knowingly or unknowingly was making Audrey's dream come true. If it were to say in Alex's voice, efforts like this deserved women to wake up from gave and cradle to his bed. Yes, Alex was doing it, and in fact he was nailing it, only if one didn't included the idiotic act of kidnapping Commissioner's daughter. The city of Angelano had now got divided into two set of people, one those knew that Rubin was now arrested, and the other those knew that Rubin was arrested but hero behind it was Alex. The second set of people were living in unofficial understanding, but for Alex it was a good PR. As if when he would appear in court, he would have public sentiments by his side.

But presently Rubin who was rotting in Police Headquarter prison cell, was in no mood to stay quiet. Larry had just hired handful of more lawyers, to work on this lawsuit, while Alina had just acquired a local newspaper to publish all good deeds of Rubin and distribute the copies for free. One of his close men approached Rubin while in cell. Rubin said, "Now what else had gone wrong apart from your pig face."

Rubin's man said, "Boss, we have tried our best with the judge. But he says, Rubin is going to pay for his crimes, and he means it. He is asking for freaking 6 million dollars for bail. It's now your call boss."

Rubin yelled, "Is he freaking insane, I mean I don't crap gold. Ah. You know what, give it to him."

Rubin knew that if Police got his further custody, they would break him by tit or tat, and getting out on bail was best bet he had. If he would be out, he will be able to deal with these greedy judges, break the witnesses, and most importantly get back to that Alex. The money was paid to the judge and Rubin got bail. To witness his bail, Alex was right there in the courtroom with his hoodie on. The entire Govt. of Angelano was on sale, and maybe Alex too could have bought his freedom in the first place only if he had dirty money, but sadly he only was in possession of dirty undies that too few of his, and few of hers. Alex knew that Rubin would be broken by now, and of course it was visible on his face in courtroom on how scared that big man looked. Rubin was getting back in his car and Alex gave him a call, a call to let him know that it wasn't over yet.

Alex said, "Wow Rubin, I am flattened to see how you straighten everything. So why don't you do the same with Audrey's death, admit it, go to prison for a day and get yourself bailed out. Simple."

Rubin snapped back, "Guess what Audrey is feeling lonely up there, time for some company."

Alex said, "Oh trust me Rubin, my memories are far greater fun than my company, and she has a share of them. But why am I telling this to you, won't you too have some of my fun memories."

Rubin yelled, "Listen you prick, you are so dead that you won't be able to regret it."

Rubin hanged up the phone. He was looking distressed, and helpless for a while. In fact a whole new game was running behind the scenes. Rubin's men who had never doubted his prowess had now got into a self-doubt. They were not able to believe that one man on a run from Police had shaken up city's biggest illegal empire. Rest of the damage was done by people whom Alex had dealt with in past few weeks. Like the Chinese drug lord Chih Ming Ho, who was not stopping praising Alex's acumen of being city's best drug dealer. Then there was Lawrence who was telling people that this man Alex is made of steel whose hand didn't shivered for a bit when hiring a killer for city detective. The computer market fiasco, well now many had known that Alex got himself hacked into bank of Bahamas without fearing the Government. Then that man who had seen Alex in the ship when loading cars, was not stopping retelling how this man Alex won his trust. The young boy who had given testimony to Alex about under age selling of liquor had quitted drinking and started an advocacy group in his college about Alex being innocent. Then that father of a young boy peddler had just started his own drug business with a firm believe that his boy wouldn't end up in ebony coffin with all thanks to Alex.

Alex was not only becoming a hero of the city, but he was also becoming hero amidst all villains of the city. In fact there was a little rumor in Rubin's camp that few people wanted to join Alex and start their own illegal business. After all Alex was the only man who had fooled the police for so long. This thing, nobody told Rubin, but Rubin knew what exactly was happening.

Larry said, "One more lawsuit, one more bail, and we will be on verge of bankruptcy."

Rubin said, "Yeah I know. This punk is causing too much of trouble. Kill him. Yes, kill him before this day ends."

Larry said, "I am sorry Rubin, but to kill him, first we will have to find him, and you know what even Police has no clues to where he could be, and as of now we are hell lot outnumbered than Police. Getting it."

Rubin said, "Okay, if not him, then kill his family, or they too are on a run."

It had to get here, especially when you were dealing with Rubin. But Alex had no idea, that his acts could get his family in trouble. All of the trouble they had faced were few random girls showing up their door and abusing Alex. But this was about getting Alex's parents killed. Alex was working on bringing down Rubin down to ground, while Rubin had just made his way to destroy Alex's world. I mean seriously, if one were to trust all those movies and books where criminals had high ethics to not bring family in between, this was just ridiculous. But none of it mattered, if Rubin had saw and read those movies and books or not.

On Rubin's order Larry had contacted few of his Latin men to do this job, well these Latin men were freelancing criminals. Larry knew that after the death of his parents Alex would not stay quiet, and if one of close men of Rubin did this, there was risk of Rubin getting into another legal wrangle, so Larry chose these Freelancers. Seriously, was there even freelancing in crime, in fact most of the crime world worked on freelancing. These four Latin men were hardened criminals and on many occasions had done handful of drug deals for Rubin. They were loyal and would commit no mistake. Larry called them in his office where Rubin too was there but getting himself a massage.

Larry said, "Two people, Steward and Martha. Kill them, burn the house, and leave no trace."

The Latin man said, "I can leave no trace even without burning the house."

Rubin gestured to Larry who said, "Oh sure you can. But you won't get as much money as without burning the house, of course after killing them. Did I made myself clear, and this needs to be done today."

Yes Steward was Alex's father and Martha was his mother. They both were retired and were living in Tantown, spending the rest of their days under the sunshine. The recent happenings in their son's life had disturbed them, but their faith as a parent was too strong on their son, and they believed that Alex had done nothing, and soon he will be as free as before. The media of Tantown had tried taking their interviews to create some spicy gossip, but on all occasions Steward managed pass through, like he asked Phone number of one female reporter so he could give to his womanizer son, etc. etc.

They might have been in the last of phase of their life, but the point was that they still loved it, and more they loved their son. If someone was to tell them that they needed to die, for their son to live, they would tell that man to jerk off because they would rather see their son live till their last breath. They enjoyed being a parent, but these last couple of weeks were too stressful. They had no idea, that someone had jerked on their life plan, and it might have been their last day on earth. The Latin men had taken a cab and tirelessly travelled all the way from Angelano to Tantown which was 300 miles far. It was evening and Steward had just risen from his afternoon nap, grabed himself a cup of coffee and was sitting in house porch.

Steward said, "Ah, wish I was younger to help Alex down in this voyage of innocence."

Martha said, "Be careful what you wish for, it is lot of trouble our son is in."

Steward picked a magazine and said, "Martha, he is our son, and it is our trouble."

The Latin men stood in the backyard of their home and watched them talk. They waited for these two oldies to step back in. Creating a crime scene on porch would be the last thing Rubin would want. The Latin men even laughed amongst themselves, as these two were older than their names. I mean they couldn't even walk properly, so running out from these Latin men was out of question. They smiled at their fate for such an easy catch. One of the Latin had even peeped through windows to check if there was someone else in the house. Clearly these Latin didn't knew that Alex was their son. In fact it didn't matter to them who was their son, they were cruel, brutal and would do anything for their existence and money. On the other hand Alex was talking with Nathan, they had a new plan, and wanted Julia to help them. Alex was completely unaware that few goons of Rubin had reached his parental house.

Steward picked the newspaper and went inside. These days, the only thing he thought about was Alex. As a father, he was in dilemma whether he did good as a father by allowing his son to become a womanizer. Maybe Steward should have stopped him, when Alex used to arrange group studies in the house consisting of only girls. Nah, that was normal, but hitting club for getting laid every other Saturday was not. Steward thought maybe he didn't loved Alex much to push him to look for immediate satisfaction from outside world. Both Steward and Martha had turned the Television on to watch some daily soap, yeah they avoided News just because of Alex. The door slammed and Latin men rushed inside, they took out their gun, while other man closed the doors and windows.

The chief of Latin's said, "Hey, nobody will act smart, except us. Ah, you two just stay where you are."

Steward said, "I don't need to act smart in front of a person who haven't taken IQ test in entire life."

The chief of Latin's laughed, "What a spirit you got, I am sure your god will like it."

Steward looked at Martha who said, "You look famished. It must have been a long day. I have some dinner prepared, so why don't you take a bite first, as anyway no one is going to have dinner tonight in this house, right."

The other Latin man said, "Bonum Est. Nobody will dine, except us."

The chief of Latin's sat at table opposite Steward while his other men went to kitchen with Martha to bring the food. Steward had known that these men were Latin, and also that they were probably been sent by Rubin, but he just needed to confirm few things, before these Latin's took blind shots. Surely the food had bought them some time. The food came in and these animals jumped on it, with guns pointed at Alex's parents.

Steward said, "Ah, as you are the last people I will meet. I need to know who are you?"

The chief of Latin men said, "Argh, I know one thing, you did something bad to Rubin, so he is doing a lot bad to you. The food is good, and for this hospitality I will say a prayer on your dead bodies. Cool."

The day had ended, and Rubin had drank champagne with Larry and Alina on the news of Alex's dead parents. The new days had begun, and there was a winning smile on Rubin's face. Seriously, no one can just walk into Rubin's life, piss on his business, and walk out with the pissing thing back. It was Rubin, and you can't just mess up with him. Rubin had intentionally told his close men to put the word out on streets that Rubin had got Alex's parents killed. This way he would win back his old fear amongst men, and people will know that Rubin forgave nobody. As for Alex, he would get to know that his end days are coming closer soon too. Rubin had even hired few more Latin goons, for killing Alex. Yeah, Latin because they were untraceable, and no one would link them back to Rubin. Larry was back in business, and had also met the judge to convince him to take some money and let Rubin go free, while Alina was trying her best in buying media to cover up for all this fiasco.

Everything was going fine. This morning felt like good old days, when on every sneeze of Rubin, his men killed his enemies. Then came the Police, not one not two, but dozens of them along with FBI, walking straight into Rubin's office. Wait what was that.

Rubin said, "Hey, hey, hey. Now what are you doing here. I didn't kill Alex's parents."

The Police Officer said, "Yes we know, you didn't."

Rubin snapped back, "Good, then what brings you here. Free Booze?"

The Police office chuckled looking back at the federal agents. He went forward and handcuffed Rubin, while others started escorting him out. The officer said, 'You have all rights to stay silent.' Everybody got off their feet, thinking what was happening. Did Alex do something else, to make life worse for Rubin. Outside the Hotel was media surrounding in hordes. They were reporting live, and Rubin thought, was Larry and Alina sleeping together rather than getting him out of this mess. Seriously was this how some of the most paid executives in Angelano worked. The Police Headquarters had many high ranking officers, and few of them appeared to be from some different departments. For the first time in life Rubin was facing such embarrassment. Detective Joe Winslow approached and took over Rubin to interrogation room.

Rubin said, "Don't tell me, Angelano PD has filed another lawsuit against me."

Joe said, "Partly yes, partly no. You are being charged with illegal immigration of Latin's, giving them unlawful shelter, and hiring them to kill innocent citizens. This is huge Rubin, even the Homeland people have filed lawsuits against you, so has Department of Illegal Immigration. You have picked the wrong people Rubin."

Wait, this time it wasn't Alex, but senior Alex. Last evening Rubin had called his Latin men when they were having food, and the Latin's told him that the work is done, as they were anyway going to kill Steward and Martha. But Steward, got to know that they were illegal immigrants, and he proposed them to become Govt. witnesses and Steward would get them Work permit. Wait, Steward could offer them such a deal because he was ex director of Department of Illegal Immigration with friends still at high places. Clearly Rubin had picked the wrong people, by all means. He was totally screwed, as top notch officers of Illegal Immigration Department took this attack personally.

Larry and Rubin were so confident of themselves that they didn't even bother to know what Steward did before retirement. In fact, they made it easy for Alex. As of now Rubin was surrounded with worst of lawsuits in Angelano Judicial history. Media was going mad, they had aired a documentary on Steward's life who was once in army and had served several wars. The soldiers association of Angelano had also stepped in, demanding execution of Rubin, or handing over of Rubin to Armed Forces Judiciary.

Finally the supporters of Alex were coming out, saying that Rubin is the killer of Audrey and now was feared of being exposed so was trying to wipe off Alex. Things had started working. Finally the smile that every club girl yearned for was coming back on Alex's face. He was talking with his father on phone, who himself was sitting in Angelano Police Headquarters.

Alex said, "Dad, I am thinking of surrendering to Police. I just can't afford to lose you."

Steward said, "Don't you dare think like that. You know why I never stopped you from hitting on girls, going to clubs, and having relationships shorter than the word itself, because deep down in your heart, you are a good man, a man though, but a good one. Son, there is no life without war, and I just can't afford to see you lose."

Alex said, "Ah, I am tired of trying, but this Rubin just won't confess."

Steward said, "You used to hit clubs, every weekend, but did you scored every time. Hmm".

Alex had got his answer, while bunch of policemen kept staring at Steward knowing he was talking to a fugitive. But come on, he was Senior Alex, and what else could you expect. Meanwhile Rubin couldn't still believe himself that he just attacked a federal retiree. I mean seriously, in all of this world, he had to be Alex's father. Couldn't Alex be a foster kid with drug abuse parents who didn't gave a damn about their kid, but wait then attacking the parents would have made no sense. Whatever it was, Rubin had really picked the wrong man, by all means. He was started to feel scared again. Soon the word will again be out on streets that Alex and his father both nailed Rubin. For a minute Rubin felt like a High School girl who was been bullied. Then came Larry to meet him who had regret in his eyes, and a face like one would make on last day of this earth.

Rubin said, "Larry please tell me something good that I got bail. God this is prison not hotel."

Larry said, "Hotel, yes Hotel it is. The judge has gone completely crazy and this time for your bail he wants our All Season hotel to be transferred to his wife's name."

~~

Chapter 17

Seriously a hotel in lieu of bail, Rubin had never thought he would lose his hotel to a young reckless boy. Alex had hit Rubin where it hurt the most. Rubin was totally losing it thinking if this Judge is taking a hotel for a bail, what would he leave for Rubin to walk free. Well for records, the All Season Hotel was one of the gems Rubin had. In fact due to its location in the commercial district, many CEO's and top Govt. Officials stayed there, with possibility that Judge must also have spent a night, and now he wanted it all. Well losing hotel was better than staying Police custody, because these lawsuits were going to last for months and months. Rubin had a reputation to save. He cannot be sharing cells with pickpockets. For the first time in life, all the crimes Rubin did were haunting him. The prison food tasted like cocaine, while the water served tasted like cheap illegal liquor. The pictures of brave policemen hung on the opposite wall appeared as if they were smudged in blood.

Everywhere Rubin looked, it made him feel like a criminal. Rubin had wiped many families that went against him, but this Alex and company has uprooted all his prowess. Rubin gave a nod to Larry and his bail was arranged. Many policemen knew that Rubin had just lost a hotel, and it was evident on their wicked smile. To Rubin it appeared that these policemen were soon going to come after his other hotels and clubs, and it was all because of that Alex.

Larry said, "Rubin, remember Big Joe, and how you wiped him off the city to claim your destiny."

Rubin said, "That was easy, and anyways he wasn't as big as his name."

Larry said, "All I want to say is, nothing is permanent Rubin and you got to embrace the change. I know this Alex isn't a big shot, but he has cost you your fortune and your business. It's time that you hear him out, not take him out."

Larry was right, even Rubin knew that but it was now that Rubin realized it. For now he was not just a womanizer, but a trouble maker for Rubin. Every man in this world was capable of doing anything, and Alex was that perfect every man. Rubin thought that maybe he should talk about settling terms with Alex, and just put a stop to all of this. Larry gave him a cellphone to make call to Alex. He called.

Rubin said, "This has to end Alex, because we both love what we have got."

Alex said, "Nice to hear that. Okay, so you confess to the Police that you killed Audrey, Terry, and it ends."

Rubin sniffed, "Listen I am not confessing anything, so let's figure something else out."

Alex said, "Nah that makes me think that you don't love what you have got. After all this, either I can go to jail, and you stay out, or I stay out and you go to jail with all the left booty to enjoy when you return back. And Rubin, I am not going suffer for what I haven't done, but you for sure will suffer for what I will do."

Rubin snapped back, "Unbelievable, you think I killed Audrey."

Alex said, "You are the drug lord, and she was covering a story on you. Who else I should expect."

Rubin chuckled, "You are so mistaken boy. I neither killed Audrey nor Terry. And do you want to know who the drug lord of Angelano is, M2 aka Morose Mamba. He is a ghost, and no one has seen him. He operates in shadows, alone, and he is the person behind all drugs smuggled in the city, no, in the state. You are so mistaken, if you really want confession, then catch Morose Mamba. Not me, I am just a small drug supplier, and you know how many other businesses i have. In fact If you need any help in catching M2, then I am here, but leave me out of your games. If you still think I am lying, then ask Joe, or your friends at high places."

Rubin hanged the phone, while pushing Alex into his thinking cap. What was that, another name, Morose Mamba, who the hell was this man? Seriously, was Rubin lying and trying to get rid of Alex by putting the blame on another person. One thing was sure that Alex had never heard of this name. But it was also sure that Rubin do was a small time drug supplier. Alex thought, oh God, now another drug lord was in picture. The first thing Alex did was do a Google search of Morose Mamba. Oh no, there it was around 10234 results by this name. He read few articles that stated, Morose Mamba was the shadow behind all drug activity in Angelano. There was also an article that had testimony from an arrested drug supplier that he got all the drugs from Morose Mamba.

Wait, if Morose Mamba was the ultimate drug lord, then why was Audrey doing a story on Rubin. Maybe Alex didn't really got all her research work, as of course women were good at hiding, like a whole make up kit in handbag. Or, Audrey wanted to get to Morose Mamba by the route of Rubin. What had felt to be finished, was just another step to catching Audrey's killer. But now how would Alex find Morose Mamba, a person who was a ghost, whom no one had seen, it wasn't even sure if this M2 resided in Angelano, or where would his base be. Alex then called Delvin.

Alex said, "Hey Delvin, have you ever heard of Morose Mamba aka M2."

Delvin said, "Oh, you can only hear about him, as nobody has ever seen him. Yeah, he is the drug kingpin."

Alex damned himself, "F, F, F. And all this time I was trying to bring Rubin down. Hey if you knew about M2, why didn't you told me. I hope you don't work for him."

Delvin said, "Come on Man, you never asked. I believed you, that Rubin killed Audrey."

Alex said, "And now I can't believe myself. Anyways will call you again, bye."

Seriously the drug kingpin, of whom no one talks about, What the F, was entire city of Angelano conspiring against Alex. Seriously catching M2 was going to be worse than a blind date. For a minute Alex even pitied Rubin who had lost more than half of his fortune because of Alex, but then he deserved that, but wait Alina didn't deserved that, in fact Alina did deserve a man like Alex, and he promised himself to make it up to her soon. Another thing which had gone completely upside down was Alex's plan that he had made for Rubin. With the news of M2 Alex was not only agitated, disappointed at himself, but also was feeling little cheated. The reason was, that if everybody knew that Morose Mamba was the drug kingpin, then why was the Angelano PD blaming Alex to be the drug Lord. He felt targeted, and in impulse made a call to Detective Joe Winslow.

Alex said, "You knew it wasn't me. But still you sold me as Angelano's Drug Lord. You know what, Audrey was right, maybe the police too works for M2 aka Morose Mamba. Yes I know about him."

Joe said, "Calm down boy, We do know about M2, and the point is that you too could be M2. That's it."

Alex said, "You are right anybody could be M2, even you too. Or maybe your 22 something son, who has been running this drug racket for last 10 years. You know what, during all of this, I have become a little good in screwing people. I am sure you enjoyed what I did to Rubin. Just wait for my next target."

Joe yelled back, "Ha I am amused. But I am sure my son has better luck than yours. See you soon Alex."

Alex damned himself. This Detective was smart, and maybe he was right too about how unlucky Alex was. For a minute Alex thought if everybody in Angelano be as scared of Alex as Rubin. It would have become so easy to prove himself innocent then. For now, Alex had no clue were to start, I mean where he would find this Morose Mamba. He was nowhere and everywhere. Alex didn't knew if this M2 had any friends, or if this M2 had any mistress, or if M2 had any holiday home, or least if he had any bank account. For now this Morose Mamba was just a name stuck between Alex and his freedom.

But wait, what if M2 had his men working in Angelano, maybe Alex could find them. But then, Rubin told him that M2 worked alone. Shit, this looked like a dead end. After coming so close to bust this drug lord, Alex was feeling helpless. Seriously, he didn't even knew if M2 hit clubs for girls, where he could get hold of him. This M2 could have been anyone, or even some one that Alex knew by other name. But then he had to start somewhere. So he sat thinking what would M2 like the most, of course money, lots of money, and he would never keep that money in banks of Angelano. Shit this was going nowhere. M2 was just a hidden identity, and nothing else. Wait, that was it,

M2 was the drug kingpin of Angelano, and he would like most to be as it was. Alex called Edward.

Alex said, "Hey, before I say anything else. Why didn't you told me about Morose Mamba aka M2."

Edward said, "Alex, there is no point in talking about someone who might even not exist. Few years back, a reputed journalist wrote a story about him stating that M2 is a cover up used by city's known drug lords, just to keep the police confused. And frankly there is nothing more to him than that name, to tell."

Alex snapped back, "Right, there is nothing more to him than that name. So why not lets have it."

Edward said, "Ah, Alex what if there is someone behind that name, and he comes back to you."

Alex said, "Come on, I don't give a F. Police already has accused me of being Drug Kingpin. So I am the M2."

Edward said, "Trust me, you are more happy with what your father named you. Anyways, what can I do?"

Alex said, "A lot, in fact you are the best help I got. I know what great network you have of reporters. I want you to tip them all, including social media influencers, that Alex is Morose Mamba aka M2. This is a story everyone will like, especially when no one knows who M2 is. Just make it official. And yes do not worry about the police that is going to go nuts after reading this. I hope you can do that."

Edward tried putting some sense into Alex, that this was a disaster move, no matter what plans he had, because it was lately that people of Angelano had started developing soft sentiments for Alex after he nailed Rubin, and this story was about to destroy it all. But Alex had made up his mind, in fact he had started to suspect himself that he was liking this shady life, with no one to answer, no one to owe for, and rule in the hearts of brotherhood. Wait, brotherhood be better out of this.

Edward did his work, and soon all influencers of Angelano had a tweet or a post about Alex is M2. In fact it got trending the #AlexIsM2. The story was soon all over the place, and mainstream media publishers were picking it for their prime time. Some were running exclusive stories on Mysterious life of M2, while others were running story on how a marketer has fooled everyone and remained the drug kingpin of Angelano. The word got out on streets as well, and all the admirers of Alex were pumped with new jolt of energy, and intent to join their new lord of the streets. In Police Headquarters Detective Joe had already called a quick meet up to make agenda of prioritizing the catch of Alex. While teenagers of Angelano, had started talking about how cool this M2 was, regardless of the fact that they haven't ever even seen cocaine. M2 was no longer a ghost, but was back in action with its new holder of name, Alex. Nathan called Alex.

Nathan said, "You are such a liar. Do you even consider me as a friend?"

Alex said, "Nathan, this was necessary, and trust me, this is what can get me out of this mess."

Nathan said, "What mess, you have been running a multi-millionaire drug racket, and still you gifted me a shaving kit on last Christmas. Seriously man, and then you always seek my help."

Alex exhaled, "Ah! Thanks for the reminder, because I seriously need your help."

On the other hand, Rubin was not much surprised to hear this. He very well knew that Alex must have had some game plan in his mind. In fact he pitied on the real M2, who was soon going to be begging for his status from Alex. Wait Rubin didn't begged of anything from Alex, the solution to their conflict came out of mutual understanding. Meanwhile the FBI and DEA had picked this story of Alex is M2 and they had stormed Angelano with quite lot of force in order to catch Alex. For long M2 had kept FBI and DEA confused and dazed, and this was now their time for the payback. The entire city had got moving, but Alex hardly cared for anything. He was sitting on a cozy bed in a hotel at shady old district of Angelano, without even one worry. Regardless he was the real M2 or not, but he did had become a hardened criminal, well not criminal, but a hardened buster. A phone rang on the cell phone.

Voice from other end said, "Finally I know who the M2 is, the great M2, who never gives a clue. Hey it's me Papa Johnny, Just wanted to hear your real voice not the dubbed one. Hey, you know what, now this Govt. will fear you more, as they will know whom they are dealing with."

Alex said, "Hey Thanks John. I don't give a F to Govt. Why not let's talk business."

Papa Johnny said, "Ah, Atta boy, always on point. That's why I love you. You know what from now, we will double our business. I have heard, the streets are going mad over you. This is the time M2, ah, Alex."

Alex said, "Okay so we will double the business. How much you got?"

Papa Johnny said, "Ah, don't worry about it. I am sitting over 600 Kg of fresh cocaine."

Alex smiled and said, "Hey John, I want it all in Angelano by tomorrow."

They hanged up while Papa Johnny was still going crazy over the fact that M2 finally was revealed to the world. For Alex the plan was working, and it was working like a charm. He hadn't expected it to be that easy, but thanks to M2 who used dubbed voice to speak with them so now they couldn't identify Alex's voice. Plus it appeared that M2 had made some good relationships with these people, I mean within a minute of conversation, the other man was ready to ship 600 kg of cocaine without one question. Now keeping that cocaine safe in the city was another herculean task, but Alex had got it covered.

Remember he speaking with Nathan about a help. Well Nathan handled the admin section of High Rise, and he also handled few of Christie's personal chores. Recently Christie had bought a new house, of whose renovation was assigned to Nathan. Well the new furniture hadn't come in, but sure that house was going to become a store house of Cocaine. Maybe this was the best revenge Alex could have taken from Christie of accusing him of stealing her soaps. Just like Alex was the new pseudo M2, Christie was new pseudo partner of M2. Everything was falling in line. Then Alex's phone rang.

The voice from other end said, "All this time a 25 year old has been running us on our feet. Whoa".

Alex said, "Oh you can thank me later for keeping the family fit."

The other person laughed, "Ha, ha. Hey this is Harry Morales. You know, I always imagined that M2 would be a sick drunkard and cigar smoking old nut, who would cough out every half an hour. But look at you. I mean you are the smartest criminals of our times. But I don't understand, why were you after Rubin. He is one of us."

Alex coughed, "Ah, long story, that Rubin cheated me and I taught him a lesson."

Harry said, "Lesson, seriously, you just ripped his books apart. You are as deadly as your name M2."

Alex said, "It's nothing new in that. It's just like our brotherhood, you hit me, and I hit you harder. Well anyways, lets come down to business as usual. How much you got."

Harry said, "Yeah of course. You know, your news and those media shows have just created a good business opportunity for us. So my investors are backing me, and this time I am thinking of putting 4 million dollars. I hope you got that much stuff, as M2 is now also a marketing man."

Alex snapped back, "I am texting you my bank account no, and this is not a promotional message. See ya!".

Alex exactly knew what he was doing. This was dangerous and no doubt deadly as well, but lot better than rotting in prison. Like if Alex had many choices. The game Alex had started was going of well. In fact, in middle of all this, Alex had also managed to open an account in Bank of Bahamas, and this money from Harry was going to end up in it, without any trace left for FBI or DEA or even Police. But seriously this drugs business was hell lot of money, 4 million dollars, I mean who buys cocaine of that amount, unless you got to feed the entire nation. In that much money, Alex could have bought himself a lifetime holiday package with any girl who liked travelling. Hell yes, and this was not going to stop, unless Alex had real M2's collar in his hands. Calls kept coming in.

"Hey, here are my 3 million dollars, but I need your best stuff, Alex. Now you have two names to save."

"Come on, I will never refuse you, except if it's about my back. Consider 300 kilos done."

~~

Chapter 18

Shakespeare argued 'What's in a name', guess he hadn't heard about M2 aka Morose Mamba. Well everything was in this name, money, good relationships, fear, power, and of course interest of all security forces of nation. For now all of this had belonged to Alex. The plan had worked, by stealing M2's name, Alex had ripped him overnight. This identity theft had worked like a charm, especially when no one knew nothing about M2. For a minute Alex thought, why didn't anybody else tried it, and looted the infamous drug lords of county. But wait, not before today anyone was as screwed due to drug lords like Alex. Yeah that made sense, in fact Alex's making of M2 was all credited to the Media, Police, and people of Angelano.

For the first time Alex realized that becoming a clean man was way difficult, than becoming city's most infamous person, but Alex was still happy with his share of mayonnaise. On the other hand, Christie's new house was totally filled with packs of cocaine. Her bed, her couch, her wardrobes, her toilet seats, her Television cabin, her shoe rack, was all so stuffed. Seriously for a second Alex thought, when all this will be over, he will tip police that Christie was ex wife of M2, who killed M2 and was now running the business. Maybe then she would know how it felt liked to be accused of being a drug lord and a soap stealer. But wait, how will then Alex would ever take Christie out, anyways that wasn't happening soon. Meanwhile FBI was interrogating Steward, as they were sure that Steward knew where Alex aka M2 was.

But Steward had made it very clear to FBI agents by saying, "Last time I saw M2, I almost cried. Yeah the reviews for Mama Mia was so right. You should see it too.'.

Steward was really hard to crack, I mean he was balls behind Alex aka M2. Alex knew the time had come to prove himself innocent, after this jolt the real M2 would do anything to save his back. Alex had his cell phones placed right in front of him. With calls coming in, of drug dealers who wanted to speak with the man behind name M2, Alex was waiting for that one call. Another call came in, and Alex said Hello.

The caller said, "Ah, it's nice to hear back from myself."

Alex smiled, "But you know what, it's not nice to be blamed for things, dirty things that you didn't do."

Real M2 said, "Hmm, that is absolutely right. But I also assume, that it must be so so nice, to have millions of dollars to one's name. But what I couldn't understand was, what will tons of cocaine do for you. I mean you seriously have a cold nose for cocaine, and you can't even cook anything with that."

Alex said, "I have already cooked something, but you seem to be not liking the taste of it."

Real M2 said, "Okay, maybe for the change of taste, we should meet, tonight. And I bet you want to."

The meeting was fixed, and Alex chose the football stadium of Angelano as meet up point. In fact the precise meet up point was the middle of ground. He had already got M2 on his knees, with 12 million dollars in an off shore account and 1200 kilo of cocaine due on M2's name. To be on the safer side and get real M2's confession, he had taken help of Marvin to hack the cameras of stadium and shoot everything when they meet. This way, real M2 would never try to harm Alex, and everything he would say would be recorded to be used against him in court of law.

Finally the air felt good, to Alex, as now he was just one meet up away from freedom. He had even talked with Nathan, who had suggested that Alex should take help of FBI, and DEA and nail that son of a gun M2 with all the force. But M2 was smart and wouldn't show up if he saw a ploy. But seriously these drug lords and criminals were so sissy, I mean a chunk stolen from them would make it feel if someone has nailed their wife.

Alex and M2 had reached the stadium. They walked closer and M2 took off his hat to show his face. Wait, what, it couldn't be happening. Alex could never forget this face, and it was him. It was Mayor's own brother, Nicholas who was also a commissioner in Angelano municipality. Seriously the commissioner was corrupt, but the municipal one, and that Mayor who was yelling out his throat against Alex would now know what it felt like to be a criminal's brother. Both smiled and came closer. The floodlights went on, as Marvin did it from his computer.

Nicholas said, "It appears, not only you are famous, I too got a face value. Ha, just kidding. Now you know i am the M2, so you must also know, I have two daughters, and a lovely wife, and a normal family life. You have got something that belongs to me. Trust me I can't payback 12 million $ nor 1200 kilo of cocaine. So let's start talking, on how can I get them back, and its okay if you have already spent thousand or two. I am liberal, as you know."

Alex nodded, "Okay, its pretty simple, confess that you killed Audrey and Terry."

Nicholas said, "Okay listen, you can keep 1 or 2 million as you need, and I will get you shipped to Bahamas."

Alex snapped back, "Listen if anyone is going anywhere, then it's you to jail."

Nicholas said, "Come on, I didn't killed Audrey. That girl always thought that Rubin was the drug lord. She was never after me. You are the first one to uncover me, catch me by my tail. And I am not scared of some girl running an investigative story. And also I don't kill people."

Alex yelled back, "They didn't died sneezing, they were killed god damn it, and I am being blamed for that."

Nicholas snapped back, "Hey, just because I am a drug kingpin, doesn't means I am bad person. I do bad business, but not bad things. Listen if you still don't believe me, call your Detective Joe, I am not scared. You got nothing on me. Plus, everybody knows you are the M2."

Alex pulled his phone and said, "You know what I have Detective Joe Winslow on speed dial."

Nicholas snapped back, "Wait, come on, stop kidding around. Okay, keep 3 million dollars, and return the rest. And i will help you in fighting this lawsuit. I have good terms with everybody in Govt. My brother is a Mayor you know that. Plus just think, if I killed that girl, why would I have come here, knowing you will spit the same poison."

Alex held his head, "I am leaving, but not you, this stadium, and your booty remains with me."

For a minute Alex was scared that few of Nicholas's men will show up and shoot him in his back. But he held his heart, and kept walking, and made it alive out from stadium. He damned himself, and also thought that Nicholas couldn't have killed Audrey. Maybe he was right, that Audrey was not even after him, then why would he kill Audrey. It made sense, and it not all made sense. The plan might have worked, but the girl turned out to be lesbian, wait the point was that Alex couldn't still find the killer. But then Audrey was doing a story on city's drug racket, then who could possibly kill her and also leave a packet of cocaine, most probably a drug dealer, or drug lord. But in these last few weeks, Alex had got all drug dealers of the city on his knees, and it was none of them. Then who the hell was the killer.

Wait, Alex didn't remembered as actually what happened that night, but then there was no chance Alex could have killed Audrey under the effect of alcohol. Alex looked at the sky, and thought to himself, why god, why always me, at least show me the way. Wait, if it wasn't a drug lord who killed Audrey, then it has to be someone else, ha, of course it had to someone else, like some old enemy, or an old boyfriend who hated to see her go, or maybe family rivalry, or somebody who hated Audrey, wait, it could also have been someone who hated Alex. But there weren't much men who hated Alex, except for all the girls he had nailed and never seen back again. God this was exploding his head, and it meant Alex was again to ground zero, to start again finding the killer of Audrey. Meanwhile his phone rang. There was nothing smiley about that, as it was Marvin.

Marvin said, "Shoot me on my face. Brother of Mayor. This news will shake the city. Good Job Alex."

Alex said, "There is nothing good about it, he didn't killed Audrey, if I were to believe a drug kingpin."

Marvin exhaled, "Man you are not getting the point. You are the first man in all of FBI, DEA, and Angelano PD, who has un masked M2. You have just caught the county's biggest drug king pin, and how the hell you couldn't be happy about it, and feel proud about it. You did it Alex. And as far as Audrey's killer is concerned, he too isn't far.

If a man can bring city's top drug lords on their kneels, most of girls on bed then who the hell Audrey's killer think he is."

Alex didn't wanted to, but smiled, "Not most of the girls on bed, the best ones are still out there."

Marvin snapped back, "That's my boy. Now listen, I have some good shit quality of recording of whatever happened out there. It's safe with me, but I am also sending you a copy. Bust him whenever you feel like."

Marvin was right, who the hell did Audrey's killer thought he was, especially to Alex who had just uncovered Angelano's most wanted criminal. Everything felt like so messed that first Alex cleared his mind by saying to himself, 'Audrey was not killed by a drug lord', 'Drugs had nothing to do with Audrey's death', 'Even if I were drugged, I won't believe that Audrey was killed because of that Drug story'. It felt good, really good.

But now FBI, DEA, and even the police were after the tail of Alex, even though he didn't had a tail, but that was the problem with these security forces. Now who could kill Audrey? If it had nothing to with criminals, then it has to be someone quite close to Audrey. Wait, what if Ashley knew something that she didn't told Alex, or what if Ashley herself was the murdered Audrey. Yeah, if Ashley was hot, then Audrey too was too cuter than Ashley, and women could commit crime on this motive. Okay, so now it was meeting Ashley again, but not at all in her apartment. Last time memories had been quite bitter , and god damn this girl also kept handcuffs, perfect to be a criminal minded blonde. Alex kept an eye on Ashley, to all the people she met, and everyone that dropped by her apartment. Every morning she went to a nearby tennis court for causal practice, and it was where Alex was about to grab her by the balls, ah the tennis balls. Ashley had started practicing, and Alex sent her a message.

'I know what you did to Audrey and I want 5 grand to keep my mouth shut'.

Ashley felt shocked and texted back, 'She is gone, and I am no longer scared of it. Screw your grands.'.

Alex was watching her while hiding behind a tree, and pounced back striding towards Ashley, who barely noticed him. Alex tapped on her back. She turned and tried shouting, while Alex tightly gripped her mouth. It was morning and as far as you could hear it was only birds chirping, with no sign of any body. Ashley then raised up her hands as a sign to surrender, and tried taking breaths, while they both got at ease.

Ashley said, "Oh, I thought, you were going to keep your mouth shut. But seriously 5 grand."

Alex said, "I knew there was more than to your looks, you little scumbag."

Ashley snapped back, "Of course, I am way more than what I look, or else you would not have let me handcuffed you in my bed. By the way, you do look good without clothes."

Alex twisted her hands to make her moan, and said, "How come I not notice that you killed Audrey."

Ashley said, "Seriously, if by any chance you would have become a detective, victims would die over and over just to make their point. You are so unbelievable. I killed Audrey, yes of course, because boys liked her more. That must be your justification. Well they did, but I didn't kill Audrey."

Alex said, "Then what are you hiding, and what are you not scared of coming out."

Ashley exhaled, "Okay, okay, I will tell you, as of course I am no more scared of this coming out. Her first boyfriend was Carl, and I hooked them up together on my birthday party. That night they slept over, and next day Carl vanished. That night I had vouched for Carl, as a great man, but what she didn't knew was that Carl and I had a relationship in past, and I very well knew that he was an Alex type man. She was heartbroken, and then we became very good friends, but I could never tell her the truth about that night. So, this was my secret."

Alex frowned, "My type of man. Seriously and you think I am unbelievable, what friend does that."

Ashley said, "I know, that's why it's an embarrassing secret. But you look so screwed up. You want to find Audrey's killer right. Check with her last boyfriend Shawn, he was always too psyched about her."

What had first appeared to be short and simple, starting with whereabouts of Terry, was now becoming a never ending quest. But one thing was sure, that it was stupid to think Ashley could have killed Audrey. It wasn't stupid, but more of a missing motive. But seriously, did any of it mattered, as Alex was no soon to be appearing for Angelano Detective exams anyways.

As per Ashley this new character Shawn was one of a masterpiece. He was a soft skill trainer who gave sessions on Compassion in Day to Day lives. Obviously he was a compassionate guy, but the problem was that he took compassion very seriously. He has always believed in fairy tales of love, wait there weren't anything of such sort as fairy tales, but he still believed in it. He had met Audrey in one of his sessions, where his eyes fell on Audrey and he lost it, while Audrey too liked him, but was casual about the relationship. Though our man Shawn often used to assert

Audrey about how much he loved her. Their relationship was sort of unequal, but eventually Audrey too started developing the same emotions as he did. But soon she also realized that Shawn was too obsessive about her, and would interfere in smallest aspects of her day to day life. I mean as per Ashley they would hit night clubs, to drink strawberry shakes, because Shawn believed that alcohol affected sperm count and egg quality. Obviously this was way too much for Audrey and she broke up, but Shawn couldn't just live with that fact, and always get in Audrey's way to bring her back. Today Alex had attended one of the sessions of Shawn, and was sitting amidst the audience.

Shawn orated, "People do you know why we exist. Yes that's right, because of compassion. Imagine, if your father or your forefathers had just jerked it off, would you still be the same. I don't think so, you would have born with Down's syndrome, or would be a Mongol child, or worse have Alzheimer before you could walk. Compassion makes us the best of what we can be. Compassion is everywhere, when you pee without littering that yellow thingy around the toilet seat, it is there when you put brakes without the one behind hitting you, it is there when you hug a person without choking them to death. So can we live without compassion."

Alex murmured, 'That's it', and he passed on a chit to Shawn. Shawn opened it and took a long breath. Then he hit the podium hard, and started damning himself. Alex had written, 'I know you killed Audrey'. Shawn looked back at the crowd, and instantly noticed Alex whom he called to the back stage area.

Alex said, "Your game is done, you son of a jerk off. I know you killed Audrey."

Shawn was getting hyper and said, "I knew it was me. I mean it has to be me, who else could kill Audrey."

Alex felt confused, "Wait. You know, it was you, and no one else could kill Audrey. Enough, listen you creep, your prison mates are sure going to enjoy your sessions."

Shawn said, "Is love a crime, because it was my love that killed Audrey. I knew she would not live a day without me, but she was stronger. She lasted one month, one freaking month, without me. That was my girl, ah, my brave girl. You know what, I want this world to know, that Audrey couldn't live without my love. Wait, you see what I am going to do. Audrey, this is for you, only you, I am coming."

Shawn lifted an iron rod kept beside him, and started smashing it on his head. Seriously, Alex couldn't really believe it. He actually had to pull that rod apart from Shawn, and throw it far from him. Shawn had hit himself some real hard, and had fell sitting on ground. Alex patted his back.

Alex said, "Hey lover boy is there anything else apart from your love that could kill Audrey."

Shawn dizzily said, "Where is Audrey, Is this not heaven. Am I not dead yet."

Alex said, "Hey, hey. Look at me. The only way to immortalize your love story is to catch the real killer of Audrey. It is only then she will rest in peace. Ah rest in compassion."

Shawn murmured, "Check with her step father, Clifford. He hated her."

Alex got himself out, while the attendees of that session told Shawn that he should have been compassionate while hitting that rod. Seriously, now Audrey also had a step father. This was interesting.

~~

Chapter 19

So there it was, Audrey had daddy issues. Seriously, people with daddy issues always got themselves into trouble. I mean how could have Alex not sensed, after seeing the secret mission of Audrey. The way she was totally into and totally not into Alex, alas the root cause was here with her father. But wait, why this Ashley didn't told him about her step father. I mean this wasn't embarrassing, in fact it gained sympathy when a girl would say, I have a step father. But then Audrey didn't need any more sympathy, as after a murder you get every inch of it.

Alex was sure that this evil dad for sure had something to do with Audrey's death. As that dying psychopath Shawn wouldn't lie. Seriously, what a nut case he was, I knew it was me. Who would say that, I mean maybe some insecure man on hearing that her woman was pregnant. Apart from getting into the mess of these drug lords, She sure did a right thing by breaking up with Shawn. But how could have she bear him for all that time. That girl was really special, and didn't deserve to die. Yeah, and now Alex was to bring justice to her cutest catch. Alex called Ashley.

Alex said, "Hey, why didn't you told me about her step dad. She is dead, and won't be embarrassed anymore. And you know what everybody has a daddy, good or bad, but a daddy, the real one, I mean, dad daddy."

Ashley said, "Okay, okay. My bad! I should have told you. It's just that Audrey hadn't talked with him for over couple of years, so I ruled him out. But, you are right, he was the dad daddy, and the bad one too. Plus he also had a motive to kill Audrey, and also a criminal record in past."

Alex said, "Oh, really. I thought you would tell me this, after reincarnation of Audrey. Isn't it too early."

Ashley exhaled, "Argh. Audrey's real dad, died in war, he was a soldier, and left huge fortune for the family. Her mother was emotionally unstable and this prick Clifford took advantage of it, and married her mother. They moved in and after 5 or 6 years, Audrey's mother died of a stroke that came out of nowhere. Now as per the will, everything went to Audrey. In fact, Audrey was the first daughter that gave his father, step father, pocket money. While her father fought in court to get custody of their house, and personal savings of her mother. He lost, and even threatened Audrey to her life. They don't speak much, but Clifford many a times was found stalking Audrey."

Alex said, "Ah, and the entire city thinks that I killed Audrey. You know what Ashley, you could have become a better story teller, if you'd told this on national TV. Thanks."

Now there was a father who had bitter terms with Audrey who didn't gave him his due share of family fortune. By the way, Audrey's mother had died of heart stroke, while her only ailment was arthritis. Seriously the police must have smoked that poor lady's joints, as to declare her with natural death, or it could have been Clifford who made all this look normal. Seriously, for a minute, wait, more than a minute, Alex felt pity on Audrey. God, why didn't she told him, that both her parents were dead. Maybe Alex would have treated her better, or had stayed awake all night to see through her eyes, and avoided anybody killing her, or Clifford killing her.

God, why do these girls always keep secrets, and more secrets. Maybe that night Audrey deserved someone better than Alex, someone special who could have kept her safe from sorrows and yes death too. Ah, as all these days had went by, Audrey had already made a special place in Alex's heart. I mean of all what Alex had known of Audrey, she didn't deserved such a prick step father.

Now talking about Clifford, he had a past criminal record of forgery. This might sound hilarious, but he had sold one house to four parties at the same time. Damn, this man was hell creative. He was charged with federal crime, fined, and even jailed. He had hidden this all from Audrey and her mother. But someone said it right, that glory lives by age. Now Clifford was an old man, with lesser ideas to screw someone. He was living in alone, in one of a rented apartment in old Angelano, which means he was closer to Alex than he thought. He was working as a carpenter, and everyday received abuses from his master for the odd work he did. Alex had followed him the entire morning till noon. Today he had taken a break and returned back home earlier than usual. Alex followed him back till the hallway of his apartment. Clifford entered and left the door opened. Alex followed him.

Clifford said, "Usually catching up with me is difficult, but age changes it all. Isn't it Alex."

Alex didn't expect this and said, "True. But age doesn't changes your crimes. I am sure this age must also have given you heaps of guilt to catch up with."

Clifford sat on a squeaky chair and said, "You are right and also clean. I know you didn't killed Audrey."

Alex smiled, "Oh really, I thought it was hard to guess, considering your age."

Clifford laughed, "Of course Alex. If you were the killer, you wouldn't have come to my doorstep to catch the killer of the girl whose murder you have been accused of."

Alex sat on his knees in front of the chair, "Listen you prick. Right now I feel like crushing your neck, and become what everybody thinks of me. But this world needs to know, that there are dirt fathers like you. Now listen very carefully. I am calling the police and you are going to confess your crimes."

Clifford burped, "And what makes you think, I killed my daughter. Ah, there do is dirt in my eyes."

Alex snapped back, "I know that, for that house, and money left after by Audrey's mother."

Clifford picked a file from tae beside him and showed it to Alex, "The house is already mine, and as you must have noticed while catching up with me that I am making money the hard way to sustain my retirement. Ah, you disappoint me Alex, a good Detective must prove a motive behind a murder."

Alex felt little shocked and said, "How did you tricked this house to your name."

Clifford said, "Ah, all these years I was chasing my daughter for this house. But it came right to me. Audrey named the house to me, with full conscious. You know she didn't liked my dirt, in fact the dirt I was living in. I might have been a bad father, but she was always the prettiest daughter of this world. So, your theory collapses here. And I feel angst whenever I think she is dead. I know I'm not much of help, but anything for my daughters due justice."

Seriously, Alex couldn't believe that all of this was happening to him. I mean all the drama, al the thrill, all the suspense, all deception, all the crimes, all the glory, all in these past few weeks. This man Clifford, couldn't even cut an apple with a knife without shivering, and Ashley felt that he could have stabbed Audrey. Wait, even Alex thought that, but then he hadn't seen Clifford before, this common sense was due on Ashley. Whatever sense was that, but this man was clean, and on top of everything, he didn't had motive, and he was so true about that. What felt the best to Alex was that Audrey didn't had daddy issues, yeah she might have been little insecure, but then lastly she was a kind girl, a girl who would gift her ancestral house to a step father who never did a thing right to her.

Seriously if god would have granted a wish to Alex, all that he would have asked was Audrey back, so he could hit more on her, take her out on dozen of dates, and of course who wouldn't like sleeping with a girl like that. In fact Alex would feel safe sleeping with her, because this girl would never take anything from anyone. And damn somebody had killed her. Alex felt exhausted, as he was again back to ground zero. Who the hell was this killer, no traces, wait there were traces of sperm but that was worth ignoring, no finger prints, wait there were of Alex, no eye witness, wait there was one housekeeper that saw Alex, and purely nothing to find a tail to this. Ashley didn't do it, Shawn didn't do it, Clifford didn't do it, then was it Alex, of course not, till he was alive. Wait, even Rubin didn't do it, but had promised that he would help Alex. Alex called Rubin.

Alex said, "Rubin, I suppose you are a man of your word, though never mind of all those occasions where I made you feel like a wimpy girl. But the point is that I need your help, and we need to find that son of a gun, who killed Audrey, and made your life miserable. Hey you there."

Rubin said, "Yeah, yeah. Of course I will help, and a wimpy girl can't say a no to a dude like you."

Alex said, "Ha, you got me this time. Now listen Rubin, I want details of all people that were there that night in your hotel and on Floor on Fire. I know that will be a huge list, so I need Alina on this, she is smart, well not smarter than me, but good enough, and also your street power."

Rubin said, "Oh, my men would love to, but I am not sure about my woman, I mean Alina."

Alex said, "Ah, how bad tables can change, now I feel it. Anyways I think men will be enough for now. Ah, that's so not me. But thanks a lot Rubin, this is the right way."

So there it was, the most infamous people of Angelano had turned into detective. Rubin was right, that Alina didn't volunteered for it, as of course there could be nothing more despiteful than a cheated woman. I mean, women always take it too personally, while they shouldn't. So Alina was still in angst that someone was a better marketer than her that was what Alex thought. So Larry pulled the list, and god there were 200 people from Floor on Fire, and 80 people from that night hotel check ins. Alex had got a copy of them, along with their phone numbers, so Marvin had to come in. With help of Marvin, Alex had managed to hack into all these phone numbers, their messaging inboxes. Alex personally had checked all the messages, and some were like this.

'Hey Honey, I will be late, I am in a meeting with a client', was from Jason from Floor on Fire list.

'Hey keep the doors opened, I want you to see me coming', was from Eric from hotel.

'You know what I just bumped into a lesbian, and she thinks I am cuter than her partner. Now I am not sure, if I take this as a compliment', was from Ralph from Floor on Fire. Wait a minute, Ralph sounded like a gay name.

The messages went on, but there was not one red flag with words like murder, drugs, Audrey, or knife, or anything familiar. Everybody was talking about getting laid, or finding someone special tonight from Floor on Fire. While the people from Hotel check ins mostly talked about flight delays, and pathetic house-keeping. Seriously, pathetic house keeping, but that night the lady from house keeping had to show up only at his door. This was unbelievable. Alex started to feel that even gods had double standards.

The messages didn't helped, and Alex knew why, of course the killer won't text his buddies that Hey I am going to kill a girl. There was not even one clue to the messages they had. But wait, it clicked to Alex and he made Marvin take out the list of phone numbers that these people called that night. He did a match up with numbers of Rubin, Larry, Alina, Police Commissioner, Detective Joe, Terry's old number, and Audrey's number. After a long Alex had crossed his fingers. Wait there was a match. Yes, the alert came in right on Marvin's computer screen. Wait a minute, there were calls, but only to Terry's number from many of the visitors from Floor on Fire. Of course there had to be, Terry was a drug peddler. But that also meant, that no one on that night had called Audrey, so probably the murderer was not there on that night. Wait how that could be possible, if the murderer was not present on that night, neither in Club, nor in hotel. It made no sense, was the murderer a ghost. To kill Audrey he must have least visited the hotel, but then it wasn't necessary that he had called Audrey. But then for sure he must have his eyes fixed on them, or he wouldn't know. Alex called Rubin.

Alex said, "Rubin, it's your turn now. Tell that killer, that you still own the streets, and no one else can commit a crime till Rubin is alive in Angelano."

Rubin said, "Hey wait, I am not a Commissioning Editor of Angelano's crime. Anyways boys are on it."

For an entire day, the street power of Rubin had turned into detectives. Yes the people that ran the street had for now became eyes of Alex, and an insider news was that they were glad to prove Alex innocent. Alex had become their idol, the person who shook the crime world of Angelano. They loved it how Alex rocked and rolled. I mean seriously before this day which commoner of Angelnao has had the balls of messing up with Commissioner of Police, Rubin, and then claiming to be the king pin of city's drug Empire. He had become like a god figure to them, and of course in crime world everyone has an idol, like a favorite movie star.

The boys of Rubin were allocated different regions of the city, with list of people to watch for. They were told to raise an alert, if someone appeared to be suspicious of having committed a murder. This all arrangement was done by ever organized Larry. I mean Larry stayed awake the entire night to find addresses of these people and geo tag them. The hunt was on. Most of the people turned out to be office goers who would only abuse their bosses in lunch breaks, and by the end of day bring packed dinner for same late working boss. Few were students that did everything besides studies, but wait no sign of murder on their conscious. Few of them were not even from the city, so catching up with them was opt out.

Of these all, there were couple of them that had served term in prison, but now they had routine sessions in neighboring churches. Then there was one stalker of women, who had entire day followed handful of women, but Rubin's men found that he was a survey man who was working on women fashion research. There was not even one man who would raise an alert. This time Rubin's men got no good news for him. Rubin called Alex.

Rubin said, "Boy, the city is clean. In fact so clean that my men have started to feel dirty."

Alex said, "Rubin that is just not possible. Audrey is dead, and someone from that night killed her. The killer is for sure on this list, but only that he is showing his cleanest laundry."

Rubin said, "My boys aren't detective, but they've got a good eye. In fact the only goodness they have."

Alex said, "Argh. This cannot end like this. You know, I think the killer knows we are on to him."

Rubin said, "Well, if that was true, it would've been easier to pick him."

Alex said, "You don't understand Rubin, I am the one who is picked. That killer is ruining my life."

Rubin said, "Don't you think even I was picked. Didn't my business also get ruined. Alex this must be hard to hear, but even you did no good to me. And I think that at this point of time, when nothing is working out, you should probably seek help of Police, not my boys from street. God damn it, most of them haven't even seen school."

Alex hanged up the phone, but couldn't hang up on fact that Rubin finally said. It was the Police that could have helped Alex, the same Police from whom Alex had been running away all this time, the same police on whom Alex didn't even trusted a bit, the same Police on whom even Audrey didn't trusted a bit, the same police that was sure about Alex being the murderer. Ah, this wasn't the end Alex had imagined. But maybe the murderer was smarter than Alex, and he should deal with it. But the problem was that Alex wanted to, but this murderer was so unavailable. I mean where did he vanished. Alex remembered his father taking him to school, and was now he going to come meet Alex in prison. God, this was so not fair. I mean what did Alex's father do, to deserve such a fate of his son. All this time, Alex believed that a killer, a person with maleficent intent could not fool a righteous women loving man like Alex, but guess what, he did. That killer won, and there was no going beyond this point, every move of Alex had failed. Life had become harsher than critics of Christie.

Was this the end, Alex couldn't believe that from this day onward he will trailed in a court as a criminal. And to top all of this, now the city thought that Alex was M2. Good god damn it, what have I done, Alex thought. Alex couldn't believe that in all of this he actually kidnapped a 7 year old girl, which normal man would do that, and how would Alex explain the judge that he was trying to prove himself innocent by committing a crime. Life was so screwed for Alex. He made up his mind, that it was no more hiding, and time to surrender. Maybe he would request the court for re investigation of these murders, and maybe convince Steward to hire city's best lawyer. Alex picked his phone and called Detective Joe.

Joe said, "Oh, it is Alex. I suppose, you have some new evidences against some body, I mean 'some' body."

Alex said, "Ha ha, detective. It's sad to see that being a police man you don't admire the spirit of innocence. By the way, there is some body behind Audrey's dead body, but not me."

Joe said, "Come on Alex, it was Audrey's dead body behind your body as per Housekeeping witness."

Alex said, "Seriously I have started to believe, that all you learnt in college was, that Alex is murderer."

Joe said, "Ha ha ha. You know boy, in all of this, you have simply not let us apply our learning. Don't you agree, that it is only you running the cards and policemen behind."

Alex snapped back, "Coming back to it. I have made this call to ensure, that you still feel good that you are still the Detective of Angelano PD. I am keeping lot of faith in your abilities, detective, and I am turning myself in. Will only take 3 to 4 hours to enjoy my freedom and will see you at 8 at Police Headquarters."

~~

Chapter 20

Few hours of freedom it was. Seriously, Alex had no idea of what would happen next after surrendering to Police. One thing was sure he was about to be handcuffed, not like what Ashley and other girls in past have done. Another sure thing was an adieu to this hotel, not to another hotel room, but a prison cell. A long court trail was to follow. On a higher note, Alex had tried everything to find the real killer, but was unable to, which made him doubt, if Police would wrap up this unfinished business. Alex for the first time prayed that these Policemen turned out to be smarter than him, and see what he had missed. Alex knew that the killer must be keeping tab on all his activities, and if he had a police insider, he would be so happy to hear that Alex was finally giving up. The only thing Alex hated was giving up to a man, of course considering that the killer was a man.

I mean in all of this world, why do all screw up had to happen with me, Alex thought. Alex was scared too, because till now Police had believed that Alex was the murderer, and if they didn't find anything solid, they would again testify in court with the evidences and witnesses that Alex was the killer, and there was simply no way of stopping it. Plus that Police commissioner would create ruckus in court, of his daughter being kidnapped. This surrender was way too much of risk, Alex was putting in. But did he have a choice. Not really, but all he had was enjoying these 3, 4 hours, and not think of anything negative. He cleared his head, and made a call to Room service.

Alex said, "Hey send in some chicken soup, lobsters, big mac burgers, and some coke. Well with coke I mean Coca Cola, not the other coke. And also send me a DVD of Sunshine Convict, it's my favorite movie. And do you by any chance have a copy of Playboy, if yes, please slide it in too. And, okay, okay what else."

Room service guy said, "We aren't going anywhere sir, take your time."

Alex snapped back, "Oh so you are also room servicing time, do you charge anything for that, because I would love to have some more time. Anyways, just bring in whatever I said."

Alex hanged up and soon realized, he shouldn't have spoken like that, especially in his last hours of freedom. It was him who was accused of that murder and not that room service guy. The huge tray with everything came in, and Alex jumped on to the burger, seriously, this one could have been the last burger of his life. Wait, the judge would never sentence him to life imprisonment, oh no, he could, so Alex took a huge bite. The coke was good and fizzy, and he felt rising up in air. Alex flipped through the pages of Playboy, and couldn't help but smile, ah girls, I will miss you, and thought that maybe they should do something nasty, for them to meet up together in prison. The movie Sunshine Convict was not his favorite, but actually felt apt for the situation, so he watched it with wet eyes. Alex picked out his phone and started checking social media.

Alex murmured, "Oh Dear Social Media, you will be missed. Wait, what."

Alex fingers got moving, as he was just browsing the Social Media account of Audrey. Well for starters, it had many cuteness overload pictures of her on it, and even some sexy ones too, but not sexier than Playboy girls. But what piqued Alex's interest was a picture posted two days before the death of Audrey, with Audrey holding a pup for the picture. Well, there was nothing abnormal with the pup, but there was a comment that said, 'Wish I was your type', and out of curiosity Alex had opened the profile of the man that had commented it, and Voila it was a man named Steve who was IT Manager at Daily Mirror.

Did it rang a bell, of course it did, it was the same newspaper where Audrey worked. Alex looked out for other comments by Steve on Audrey's profile. Yes there were more like, 'You are the sexiest woman on earth', 'Ah, if beauty can kill', wait, 'Kill', it was the filter that Alex had been searching for all this time. Also Steve was an IT manager, so probably he had ability to hack into Rubin's account and make that payment of 50 grand to Eddie. This was it, maybe god had planned something else for Alex. Alex called Marvin.

Alex said, "Hey the list we had of people from Floor on Fire, just check if there is some Steve on it."

Marvin browed through his system and said, "Well he is there, on that list."

Alex exhaled and said, "Now just check if this person has some nastiness of yours. I mean check on the dark web, if this person has some hacking history."

Marvin browsed and said, "By the way I am not nasty, it is the people that make me do this that are nasty. Yeah, this man has an alias on the hacker dot net website."

Alex hanged up the phone, and strode out to drive the first thing to Daily Mirror office. This was it, he was a hacker, he was there on the night Audrey got killed, he was a colleague of Audrey, and he was also stalking Audrey on Social media. God, finally something good you did, Alex thought. But why didn't Alex first saw the social media account of Audrey, god how could he have missed this, this was a disaster. I mean all this trouble could have been saved. At last, it was again this marketing too that has saved him. God Social media was more powerful than he had ever thought of it. Alex couldn't believe that in few hours he was going to surrender himself, but now he will bring in the real killer. Ah, finally Audrey would get her due justice, and this man would pay for his deeds. But seriously Alex realized that he was not at all a good detective, and if he were he sure would have taken a look in the office of Daily Mirror much sooner than now. Wait, it was not only Alex who was a bad Detective, but Joe had failed the test too. I mean how could Joe have not noticed Steve before. So, there weren't any good detectives in whole city of Angelano. Ah, this was the reason why people like Steve were roaming free.

Alex parked his car right in front of Daily Mirror's office, and wait could that be true, Steve was standing right next to a food truck in front of Alex, getting himself a cup of coffee. Steve's eyes fell on Alex, while Alex pretended that he was just stopping by, but Steve hurriedly took the coffee and went back inside Daily Mirror's office. Alex thought, dude that is so him the killer. Alex followed him, while the phone rang and it was Detective Joe.

Joe said, "I hope you are coming right, coming to Police HQ's, because new commissioner wants to meet you."

Alex snapped back, "Oh yes Detective we'll meet, and he'll sure award me with some medal, but not now."

Joe agitatedly said, "Seriously a medal, and for what, nailing the law and order. Now you listen boy, enough we have had of you, get your back right to the Police HQ's".

Alex hanged up the phone, while Joe kept yelling. Seriously, no other criminal, ah accused criminal other than

Alex had such bothered Joe ever in his 10 year long career as a detective. Joe said to himself, Oh come on, not again. Alex went inside with hoodie on, while the day was about to end, the reporters of Daily mirror had started walking out for their home.

Alex stopped by a cubicle and picked the access card lying on the desk. He went ahead and started searching for the IT section. Alex knew that Steve for sure would be there, thinking he will be safe inside the office. Seriously, this was the place where Audrey worked in, and if she hadn't died that night, then maybe today Alex had visited this office with a broad chest in order to pick up Audrey for a night out, ah, but this Steve had screwed it all. Where was he, Alex searched the entire floor, then his eyes fell on the server room at the end of alley. There it was, the den of this murderer. Alex looked around and crept inside the server room. Steve was there sitting on his chair glued to the computer screen. Steve turned, and it was evident by his face, that he was so scared like shit.

Alex yelled, "This is what feels after killing an innocent woman. Wish you were that scared before killing her."

Steve stayed silent and Alex continued, "You thought you will get away with this, but no, you have messed up with the wrong person Steve. Being an IT guy, you should have stick to Computers, and not knives."

Steve gulped and Alex said, "Guess what, this night we are going to hit the Police HQ's, it will be fun."

Steve was falling backward with Alex approaching him, "Oh, there will be hairy men, that will shove those rods right in your back, ah, and trust me there is no climax better than this for you."

Then the door opened from behind, and a man entered. He said, "Hey Steve you all right."

Steve broke out, "Its him, he is the killer, He killed Audrey."

Alex turned around to see a smiling man, who had confidence on his face and blood drooping from his jaws, well the blood wasn't really dropping, but then this was how killers looked like. Well, this man was Jimmy, a senior journalist of Daily mirror, at least what his identity card said hung around his neck. Jimmy was a crime journalist, and often took help of Steve for hacking into these criminals personal life. In fact the story which Audrey was working into, to uncover the drug racket of Angelano, Jimmy was her helping hand in that, but if only Alex had known that, this encounter must have taken a while earlier. Jimmy slowly turned around and he locked the IT room from inside. Though Steve had loudly said that it was Jimmy who killed Audrey, he didn't looked even a bit scared. Jimmy went in and tapped on Steve's back, who was apparently a patient of bronchitis which got triggered while Alex has been accusing him. So there it was, Audrey's killer, and even a witness as in Steve. This was end of Alex's troubles. Alex was looking right in eyes of Jimmy, and Alex tonight wasn't going out of this room either without the murderer.

Jimmy said, "I was there that night in Floor on Fire, when you were hitting Audrey, and other girls as well. I saw you, in fact you are good at it, and I even felt a bit jealous, on how quick you catch the girls by their nerves. But you know what, you did wrong by picking Audrey. She was my girl. But being a man with modern outlook, I find a little flirt being okay, but then you took her to the hotel room. Whoa that is not acceptable, Alex."

Alex in fury said, "Oh don't worry, tonight I am here to hit on you, and take someplace called Prison."

Jimmy said, "Ha ha. Your fascination power is quite good Alex."

Alex snapped back, "Oh, if you don't know. I am also good at nailing, earlier women, and now criminals."

Alex continued, "Wait, you are not just a criminal, but a coward criminal, and Audrey hated men like you."

Jimmy said, "Well, not completely, she also admired me for my work. You know that night I and Audrey had drinks, and funnily we also talked about you. Everything was good, but when I asked her to sleep with me, she slapped me, seriously a slap on my butt would been okay, but she chose my face for her slap. I got mad and took the knife from table and before I recovered from that slap, she was dead. You know what, even I wanted a one night stand with her, but she chose you. It might sound odd, but Alex, we are same. We both hate relationships, we both love sexy women, and we both seek one night stands. We are same Alex."

Alex snapped back, "You are right, we are same, and maybe this society can only handle one of us."

Jimmy smiled, "Oh so rightly said, Alex. It's time for one of us to go."

With that Jimmy quickly took a LAN cable and wrapped it around Alex's neck to choke him to death. Seriously, Alex thought, what was that, were this man not going to go from this society into prison. The grip tightened, and so did the tussle. Alex tried his best of power to shrug Jimmy from his body, but Jimmy was strong. Seriously it doesn't had to end like this, didn't the villains died in the end. What was it, evil winning over the good. Well agreed, Alex was no god, but he was good at heart, and plus he didn't killed Audrey. Alex started losing his conscious, he was fainting, and just on edge to die. His hands had stopped struggling.

Steve took a keyboard and slammed it with all strength on head of Jimmy, oh yes on head of Jimmy, and yelled, "I am tired of following orders of this son of pig. Audrey was a good girl and she will get her justice."

Alex nodded and tried breathing hard, "Oh man, what took you so long, the keyboard was right there."

Seriously all good things come to an end, wait, all things come to a good end, yeah that was better. The real killer was caught. Whoa, after all this struggle, trouble, plans, ploys, evidences, running, finally Alex got his hands on the killer. Now the freedom was all his, and he could again hit clubs, but be more careful. Anyways, this was not what Alex was thinking, he was really feeling sorry for Audrey, who got killed because of a one night stand, Alex's favorite thing to do.

Well, the Police and Detective Joe Winslow have reached the office of Daily Mirror, while the other colleagues of Audrey at Daily Mirror were still in shock to know that Jimmy was her murderer. Joe had soon made him confess that Jimmy did killed Terry as well. Terry was the man who gave Jimmy the packet of cocaine that night, which Jimmy used to drug Audrey so she could sleep with him easily. When Alex approached Terry, Terry had made up his mind that after the Chinese deal, he would tell everything to Police, so Jimmy killed him too. The money transferred to Eddie's account was done by Steve, and he confessed it without anybody asking him. In all of this, girls at Daily Mirror were already asking Alex about his phone number. Wait not to hang out, but they were interested in taking Alex's interview. Well, interview was just an excuse to go out together. Joe approached Alex.

Joe said, "So, you do are the hero of the day. But I will have to arrest you too, for kidnapping Jade."

Alex exhaled and then said, "What if I give you something that makes this kidnapping, napping."

Joe said, "Hey I don't take bribes, and what else you got other than that Chinese Drug deal money."

Alex whispered, "I have 1200 kilo of cocaine of M2, and by the way Nicholas is M2, Yeah Mayor's brother. But please don't put the Govt. brotherhood in between."

Joe talked with his new commissioner about this revelation, and rest of the charges on Alex were dropped. Alex was as free as he could ever be. Soon the news got flooded with breaking story about Nicholas being the M2. Media was all over it, they even shot live Police raiding Christie's house with all that cocaine. Alex had become the official hero of Angelano, while its criminals were counting their last days. The Mayor had appeared in public and said, 'Nicholas is not my brother anymore. He is yours, all yours, and he will get what he deserves. There will be no more drugs in my city. I want each man of this city to be like Alex, well not in hitting women, but hitting the criminals'.

Seriously, Alex thought while watching the News from his own bedroom in Mr. Walters house. I mean Alex was not only about hitting women, I mean he was, but he was also a marketer, I mean why where the marketing associations not coming forward and awarding him accolades for best use of marketing. Anyways, that would happen soon too. Ah, it really felt good to breath as a free man. But there was one thing that had struck Alex hard, real hard. Jimmy had said, that Alex and him were same, and this had got Alex thinking, his craving for sex and women was the same as of Jimmy, and if Alex had to be the hero, he had to mend his ways. He couldn't be only seeking one night stands, after he took a stand for so long to get himself and a girl named Audrey justice. Alex realized he was better than hookups, and there was more to him than loose pants. Meanwhile his phone rang.

Christie said, "Oh there is my hero, you know what, take your time, unwind yourself, and then come back to office. We can't wait to have you and your wicked ideas on board again. And this is to tell you, that lately I have been thinking that we could be more than a boss and an employee. Anyways, as my new house is a crime scene now, I am up at my office condo, feel free to drop by anytime, I would love to host you a night."

Alex chuckled, "Ah you know what, I still prefer yours soaps over you."

Christie laughed, "Of course you do. Anyways, I have a whole new stock of them, in case if you need to know."

Seriously, was this some miracle that Christie called Alex to invite him to a naughty night. Wait, and why did Alex had to say that he liked her soaps over her. Well, Alex thought, it was the best thing to say, as there were no more one night stands, and for god sake, he had to work in that office for quite longer than how one night would stand. But still, an offer from Christie was no less than a marketing award, not because she was his boss, but she was quite hot. It also felt nice to have a day job back, and earn a living by respectful means. But seriously, after having got his freedom, what Alex was missing was screwing the nastiest people of town. I mean it might have happened all because there was sword hanging on his neck, but he had started enjoying it.

Outside his apartment, there were many OB vans, and media people grouped around to take his interview, seriously what else one could ask from life. Then appeared Mia on television, Whoa, Mia, he had almost forgotten about her. She said, "Oh Alex is a darling and the hero of Angelano. He has a secret crush on me. I have seen it many a times in his eyes. Hey Alex, let's go out some time. With Love Mia". Wait what, an invitation from queen of Latex dresses. This was unreal, and wait all this time she did had noticed Alex, but no, not now, I mean he wouldn't hit some cheap clubs with Mia, but rather take her to some fine restaurant for a dinner date, yeah that would be more sober. Alex then opened his mail, and there it was floods of Free club membership offers from top clubs of city. Ah, this had to happen after all this.

Nathan called, "Hey Alex. I am coming over to your house, Julia wants to see you."

Alex said, "Oh all I can give her is, mayonnaise on top of muffins, and I am sure it will really not taste well. So not now, I have some else place to go, and its important."

People were sitting in silence, while the priest read his prayers. Everyone had sorrow in their eyes, and a half hearted smile to what the priest said. This was a memorial service in memory of Audrey hosted by her father. In fact Clifford had personally invited Alex. Alex went on to the cutest picture of Audrey, kept few flowers and kissed on her forehead on picture. Seriously, Alex wished if Audrey was alive, she had to be the nicest person with whom Alex had a fling with. Her voice still echoed in Alex's head. It felt she was there somewhere watching all these people, and feeling good on how much she was loved. It was Audrey that made Alex catch the criminals, and for a minute that sounded like love, but Alex winced because it was more of a self love thing. Then someone tapped Alex from behind. Wait what, was that Audrey, no it can't be.

The girl said, "Don't be surprised, I look a lot like my sister, just wanted to meet you. You are the last person my sister was with. You are the only man who took a stand to get my sister her due justice. I want to know everything that my sister told you. Let's go out tonight, some place."

Alex smiled and said, "Ah, not feeling great to go out, but this is so not me."

The girl smiled, "Cool, then meet me at my place, i will be by myself. But I have got only this night. Tomorrow i am leaving the city."

Alex thought, wait, what, this was the third time in a day, invitation by girls. He turned around and murmured to himself, 'May be I need to reconsider my stand'.

✳✳✳